DUSTY

N.J. ADEL

This is a work of fiction. All incidents and dialogue, and all characters are products of the author's imagination. Any resemblance to persons living or dead, similar books or characters is entirely coincidental.

ALL CHARACTERS DEPICTED ARE OVER THE AGE OF 18.
WARNING
THIS BOOK FEATURES EXPLICIT DEPICTIONS OF SEX, DISTURBING SCENES AND OTHER MATERIAL THAT MAY OFFEND SOME AUDIENCES. THEREFORE, IS INTENDED FOR ADULTS ONLY.
No part of this publication may be reproduced, distributed or transmitted in any form or by any means, including photocopying, recording, or other electronic or mechanical methods, without the prior written permission of the author, except in the case of brief quotations embodied in critical reviews and certain other noncommercial uses permitted by copyright law. For permission requests, write to the author at the e-mail address below.

N.J.ADEL.MAJESTY@GMAIL.COM

First published by N.J. Adel and Salacious Queen Publishing Aug 2022. Published with a new format, size and cover Nov 2022

DEDICATION

To dominant alphas who bow to no one
But once they find their queens, they're not afraid
to submit
Knowing very well there is something extremely
hot about being under a woman's mercy

PLAYLIST

Hell to Have You by Our Last Night and Sam Tinnesz

3days by Mitchel Dae

Bad Day for My Enemies by Adam Jensen

The Rival by The Wise Man's Fear and Lauren Babic

Dolls by Rain Paris

Eros by Alura

Dangerous by Rivals

Aftermath by Massface

Monster by Fight The Fade

The Drug In Me Is You by Falling In Reverse

DUSTY

TABLE OF CONTENTS

CHAPTER 1

CAMERON

Chelsea stared at me with her nose crinkled like I were a mysterious creature with a bad smell. "What do you mean he jumped out of the window before the date was over?"

I closed my dorm room so that the whole campus wouldn't know about my epic failure and threw a couple of outfits in my backpack to get ready for the weekend. I didn't know why I even bothered telling her about my complete dating fuckups she hooked me up with when every time she'd just look at me like that and then find someone even worse to hook me up with later.

"Cameron, you're not getting rid of me that easily. You're gonna tell me everything. Now."

"You told me to be spontaneous and slutty, so I suggested bathroom sex." She had her way in making me speak anyway. She had that tone, that powerful charisma that I admired and wished to have one day.

"That's a good move, and that rasp in your voice when you're inviting is sexy as fuck. No guy would leave before he hit that ass."

"Right? Well, no. That didn't happen, and it was a terrible idea." I couldn't believe I'd even made that suggestion, but any sex was better than no sex. I was in fucking college—third year for fuck's sake—and couldn't score a date that lasted more than one night that Chelsea had to intervene and set ones up for me. Yesterday, I hit a new record, though. He didn't even finish the night.

"Are you telling me he said no? He went running for the hills rather than stay and fuck you before the date even ends? That doesn't make any sense. He's a guy about to score. He wouldn't just leave. What the fuck really happened, Cameron?"

I sighed, frustration coursing through me. "Well…he…wanted to choke me, but I laughed, probably longer than I should have. Then he spanked me, called me a naughty girl and went to choke me anyway, demanding I called him Daddy. I kinda, might have reached for his hand, twisted it and choked him instead. I think I made him cry…just a little."

Chelsea gave me the stare again but without the crinkled nose. Then she burst into laughter.

I rolled my eyes, finishing packing. "It wasn't funny, especially the daddy part."

She cut the laughter and rubbed my shoulder. "I'm sorry, Cam. I should have told him. I just didn't think it was my place to mention it."

Telling a boy the father of the girl he was about to blind date took his own life two years ago because that shit happened to veterans all the time, or so we were told, wasn't exactly a turn on. "Well, I did." Not the suicide, but the fact that Dad was a great soldier that taught me how to fight, no one would ever fill his shoes and no matter how much I missed him, I would never call anyone else Daddy. "And that's when he begged for his life because apparently I was still choking him this whole time. I tried to apologize, but the second I took my hand off his throat, he yelled, 'that bitch is trying to kill me,' and just jumped out of the window."

"I'm gonna kill him for you, babe. Don't worry about that pathetic loser," she said, snorting a laugh. "Next time, I'll—"

"There will be no next time. I'm begging you."

~ 3 ~

"You have to get laid, Cam. That dry spell isn't good for your vagina. We all love and are grateful for toys, but you need to catch a dick every now and then."

"I don't think I'm good at sex."

"Says who?"

"Every boy I've been with never came back for an encore. That says a lot."

"You just didn't find the right guy because you haven't explored all your options yet. There are so many kinks out there. I once had a guy who *paid* me to boss him around, clean up and cook for me and then whip him if he failed to make me come."

I blinked at her. "Wow. Paid you to live every woman's dream?"

"Yes, babe, and it is my mission to get you someone who makes yours come true."

I zipped my backpack. "Don't bother, Chels. I'm going away for the weekend anyway."

"Do you have to go every weekend? You're missing all the good parties."

"You know I do. My sister is everything to me." Ever since Dad, my sister, Annie, had to go live with Sylvia. I didn't trust that woman to take care of herself, let alone a fifteen-year-old girl. I wished there had been anywhere else for Annie to stay or I could have taken care of her myself. But we had no other relatives but our shitty mother, and I couldn't find a closer school to San Francisco unless I was willing to lose my scholarship at CIT.

I wished I could have afforded it, but Dad left us nothing but a small house and a Challenger. The military compensation was there to cover Annie's school and living expenses as Sylvia couldn't pay for either. My only option was to suck it up for the next couple of years, spend five days a week worrying sick about Annie and take the six-hour trip from Pasadena to San Francisco every weekend to give Annie some of the care she deserves, until I graduated and got a job. Then she'd come live with me so far away from that woman and all her shit.

My phone chimed in my pocket. I looked at the screen. It was Sylvia. "Speak of the devil." I glanced at Chelsea. "I have to take this."

"Okay, but before you go, I'm gonna bring you *something*. Take it with you and use it to get familiar with it. They'll come in handy with your next date."

That girl never gave up. Before I swore, she took off, so I glared at the phone and tapped the green icon. "I'm coming as usual, Sylvia. Already packed and have my bus ticket. Don't worry, you won't have to take care of your own daughter for the weekend."

"Uh…Cameron…" she sniffled.

A pang set in my chest. Why was she crying? What did she do now? "What's wrong? Is Annie all right?"

The sniffling turned into whimpers.

"What the fuck?! Where is she?!"

"I don't know. She… I didn't see her coming home last night, and I couldn't find her in her room this morning either. I called her right before I called you. She isn't picking up."

"What the fuck, Sylvia? I called her yesterday afternoon and she was going to get ice-cream with her girlfriends and assured me she was going straight home right after. How could you not notice she was late or didn't come home at all?"

"I thought she was gonna stay over with her friends or something, but…"

Blood pounded my skull. "But what?!"

"The neighbors said they last saw her yesterday," she cried.

Tears sprung to my eyes, too. "Where?"

"On the bike of a big, blond Night Skull."

The phone slipped from my hand as I crumbled on the bed, breaking in gasping sobs.

"Cam? Cam?!" Chelsea's voice came from a distance, as if under water, yet her hands were rubbing my shoulders and face. "What's wrong? What happened?"

Head spinning, I managed to look at her. "The Night Skulls took my little sister."

CHAPTER 2

DUSTY

My bike, I missed. This, not so much.

Wasted, old, hairy-ass men fucking like hogs in our front yard in the name of yet another club party was the last thing I wanted to come home to. I should have gotten used to it by now, born and raised in Rosewood, the estate on East Bay hills in San Francisco where the Night Skulls MC reigned, where my father was the king of this mayhem I'd soon inherit or, at least, help run. But nothing, not even the sight of the sweetbutts sauntering naked and horny, ripe for the taking, would ease the sight of the brothers' sweaty balls slamming pussy while their wrinkly asses welcomed me home.

"The prodigal son returns!"

All eyes were on me as I stood by the gate, and the brothers howled over death metal music, spilling beers and bodily fluids. I didn't know who announced my arrival. It was too loud to recognize the voice, but it wasn't Dad's. Roar was nowhere to be spotted in this orgy. It was probably Rush, the VP.

In no time, brothers and bitches swarmed around me, a prospect took my backpack to put it in my room, and a beer found its way into my fist.

"How's Europe?" one of the bitches wearing only shorts asked, flinging her hair to show me more of her than what was already on display. "Do they throw nice parties like ours?"

"What about the girls? Prettier?" another one asked. She was shorter and curvier, blonde like the first but still had her bra on. No shorts, though. Only a G-string.

The Night Skulls shared the same lifestyle, taste and business around the globe. There were nights when the club whores were into some kinky shit I didn't even know about. It was exciting at first, getting laid, being treated like a king and learning something new in bed every day, but after some time, things started to look so similar, usual, even sweetbutts. After a while of partying and fucking every day, they all looked the same.

I wasn't complaining, though. I might have been fidgeting when it came to the club…business and how it was run when I patched in after I finished high school. The bars, the gambling, even the drugs were okay for me. But not the pussy. Definitely not the killings.

Selling bitches and getting rid of anyone who dared be in the Night Skulls' way, in Roar's way, was just too much. I was raised in hell. That didn't mean I was necessarily a devil.

Roar felt my hesitation, so he sent me on a trip to Europe where the Night Skulls had other chapters to understand how important and big we were. To believe that the killings were a necessity and the pussy was a fun, easy way to make cash.

After spending the summer traveling around Europe, visiting the global chapters and partying like my life depended on it, I loosened up a lot. For a nineteen-year-old traveling the world, bitches throwing themselves at him just to win him over, an endless supply of booze and drugs at his disposal, meant everything.

I came home, ready to embrace my patch again.

"Girls, this ain't the night for chatting. Get your mouths busy doing what you do best." Doc, an ex-military doctor in his forties, and my best friend and favorite brother, winked at me. "Take them and have some fun in the back before Mama sees you. If she gets here, you won't have a moment for yourself all night, and she'll feed you all the food she's been making all day."

"She's here?" I was surprised Doc was the one who picked me up at the airport and not my mother. And if she was here, how was she not out already? She'd called me every fucking day when I was away that sometimes I had to ignore her calls; I understood I was her only son, but Jesus.

"Roar is keeping her busy. He hid the time of your arrival from her and told her to go check on the strip clubs until you came home."

"Why?"

"Beats me. He's inside waiting for you. He said he had a surprise for you he didn't want her to see."

I chuckled, as one of the girls stretched on her toes and whispered a slutty proposition in my ear, telling me she could take a ten-inch like a good girl.

I leaned in and whispered back, "but can you take it with a Jacob's Ladder and a Prince Albert while my hand is around your neck and the other fisting your hair?"

Her nipples hardened as she smiled. "Bring a belt, too."

"Oooh. You're on." I spanked her as she sauntered to go inside. I took the curvy girl, too. I loved curves.

But when I went to my room, Roar was there, and he wasn't alone.

He rose off the bed, his long, greasy, dark blond hair bouncing off his cut, and gave me a hug. "Welcome back, Son. I have a very nice surprise for you." He glanced at the bitches and dismissed them with one gesture. I was too occupied with the guest in my room to object.

"You must be tired of patch whores," he laughed. "I have something way fucking better to celebrate your return."

CHAPTER 3

CAMERON

TWO MONTHS AFTER ANNIE'S ABDUCTION

Annie's beautiful, innocent face stared back at me as I laid the stack of posters I'd been peppering San Francisco with for two months on the diner table.

"I can't believe they closed the case and set him free." Bianca, a waitress I'd become friends with at Alfarez, the diner I'd been having breakfast at every day since the abduction, poured me some coffee.

I'd waited for months for the police to do something. To bring my sister back. To search Rosewood. To interview the members of that fucking motorcycle club. To give me any form of justice. The president of the Night Skulls and his bike fit the description the neighbors gave the police, but all they did was bring him, and only him, for questioning once, and the result? An obnoxious smirk on Roar's face when he was released the very same day.

"Roar must have bribed them." A single tear dropped from my eye as my raspy voice came out overtly hoarse. "I don't care what they said. The Night Skulls have my sister."

"I'm so sorry, Cameron. I wish there was something we could do to help." She pointed at the posters. "Do you want me to post those?"

A troubled sigh burst out of my chest as I shook my head. "Thank you, Bianca, but there's no point anymore. You'd better go check on your tables. I don't want Mr. Alfarez to be upset. He's been very kind to me, letting me here every day, putting Annie's posters and annoying the customers with my questions about seeing her."

She patted my shoulder gently and left to refill coffee. I grabbed one of the posters, the fire of missing my sister blazing in my heart. What was I thinking seeking help or justice from the police that were in Roar's pocket? They would never have helped, and Annie… What were they doing to her now? "Oh my God, Annie," I broke with tears.

"Uh…excuse me?"

My head whipped to the side toward the voice. A girl my age was standing at my booth, her hair a dark ponytail and her eyes covered with sunglasses.

"I'm sorry to interrupt you, but we've met before. I study at USF. I helped with some of the posters around campus."

Her face began to look familiar. She was one of the girls that was moved by Annie's story and asked everybody on campus to help find my sister. "Yes…of course. I remember. Thank you for your help. I'm sorry I don't think I caught your name, though."

"It's Jo. Jo Meneceo."

I wiped my nose. "Thank you, Jo. Your help is truly appreciated. What's your major?"

"English. Senior year."

"I wish you all the best. I used to study Engineering at CIT. Third year."

"Used to?"

My lips puckered in sorrow. "I haven't been attending for the past two months. I'm pretty sure I lost my scholarship by now."

"I'm so sorry. Listen, I...I didn't mean to eavesdrop, but I accidentally heard you speak with the waitress about the case. May I sit for a minute?"

"Sure."

She slid into the booth across from me. Then she looked around, as if she was checking if someone was watching or listening, before she leaned forward and whispered, "If you really think they have her, the police aren't the way to get her back."

My brows hooked. "What do you mean?" I leaned forward to level with her. "Do you know anything about Annie?"

"Unfortunately not, but I know one thing. There's no authority in town that can overpower the Night Skulls but one. That is the only kind of help that will be useful to get your sister back."

My whole body buzzed with hope. "Who?"

A tight smile pressed her lips as she seemed to be contemplating her next words.

The danger lacing her caution reached me. Whatever she was about to tell me must have been hard to say. But I couldn't let her not say it. I was desperate, and I was ready to do anything to bring Annie back to safety away from those monsters. I held Jo's hand and squeezed gently. "I swear I won't tell anyone it came from you. I promise."

She nodded once. "Thank you. Can I borrow your phone?"

I gave it to her. She typed something and handed it back to me. When I looked at the screen, there was a note. All it said was *The Godfather.*

My eyes narrowed for a second. "You're not talking about watching the movie to learn how to deal with bad guys, are you?"

She chuckled. "It's a great movie with multiple life lessons, but no. I'm sure you're smart enough to know what I'm referencing here."

The Italian Mafia.

My skin broke in goosebumps just at the revelation alone. "I see. Even if I can bring myself to accept help from said authority," *as far as I understand they operate on favors, and I don't think the money I have left from the gratuity can cover. What else can I give them instead?* "I don't know how to make that kind of connection."

"It's easier than you think. You just need more coffee," she said.

I squinted at her, but then I blinked in surprise. My eyes switched to Bianca and then back at Jo. "Really?"

A softer smile brushed her lips as Jo rose. "Delete the note. If someone asked what I was doing with you, please tell them I was giving you my number in case you needed more help with the posters."

"Of course. Thank you. But…why are you helping me with something so…you know?"

"I know how it feels to lose a member of your family, the one you love the most. I don't wish it upon anyone." She squeezed my hand before leaving the booth. "Good luck, Cameron. I really hope you find Annie."

CHAPTER 4

CAMERON

Bianca Zanetti couldn't be Mafia. That kind, compassionate petite woman couldn't be connected to such a ruthless organization.

But when two particular twin brothers in expensive Italian suits and cruel tattoos on their wrists walked in Alfarez, and at the same moment Bianca was practically having a panic attack and stayed in the kitchen instead of waiting on the tables of her section all the time the twins were there, my thoughts crumbled to the ground.

Something was up with her and the twins. I needed to figure out that connection if I had any chance of asking her to help me finding Annie.

I watched, one booth away, as another waitress went to the twins' table, welcoming them back, mentioning their name. Lanza. *The* Lanza crime family that ruled over San Francisco. My salvation and only chance to get Annie back.

One of them was pissed off. "Where's Bianca?"

The waitress bent over, showing them an ample amount of her cleavage. "She's not in today. I'm covering for her."

That's a lie. Bianca is hiding in the kitchen. Why was Bianca forcing that girl to lie for her? If she's connected to the Mafia like Jo said, why was Bianca so afraid to meet the Lanzas?

"What's your name, bella?" he said.

Her shaking was visible from here. "Mona."

"Tell me, Mona. Is Bianca just hiding or is she watching, too?"

"I...I told you—"

His fist wrapped around her wrist, and she gasped. "Don't you dare lie to me again...Mona. Be honest and play along, and you have my word I'll let you go without a scratch."

"I...I...don't know if she's watching," she said.

Fuck. Should I intervene? He's threatening her, and by the tears sparkling in her pleading eyes, he must be hurting her.

Without thinking or calculating the danger I might be putting myself in, I got off my seat to help the girl no one bothered to even look her way. Suddenly, people from the other tables stared at me, asking me to stay put. Their body language screaming at me, "this is a bad move."

Then I saw Mr. Alfarez coming from the other end of the diner. He, too, shook his head at me. Then he gestured for me to sit back.

What the fuck? If he didn't want me to help, why wouldn't he? Why wouldn't anyone? Why was everybody too scared to defend the helpless when it came to the Lanzas or the fucking Night Skulls? Why would no one lift a finger to help a woman like Mona or an innocent girl like my Annie?

"Sit on my lap," the Lanza asshole ordered Mona.

"What?" she squeaked.

He forced her on his lap and ran a finger along her jaw and down to her chest. Then he leaned into her ear, whispering something. Then she was nodding with a swallow. "Yes, Cosimo. Anything you want."

My blood simmered. As he let her walk away, I realized all that power play, all the intimidation, the threats, harassing a woman, shaking her with fear to the point of crying and begging was all, obviously, an attempt to make Bianca jealous. The girl who would rather hide in the kitchen than meet him. The girl he couldn't have yet.

Cosimo Lanza had an eye for Bianca Zanetti, and he'd do anything to have her.

I wanted my little sister back, and I'd do anything to have her.

The key to saving Annie is behind that kitchen door, and I'd stop at nothing until I had it.

CHAPTER 5

CAMERON

Bianca wiped her bloodshot eyes—I'd found her crying in the bathroom—and glared at me in disbelief.

I took a deep breath. "I know I'm asking for a lot, but—"

"I'm not going to fuck Cosimo Lanza for a favor."

"Of course not. That's not what I'm saying. All I'm asking is that you give him one date in exchange for his help to get Annie back."

Did that make me evil? A terrible person to ask her to date that Mafia boss and make her ask him for a favor on my behalf? I knew I felt I was, but a guilty conscience or being judged was the last of my concerns. A trivial price to pay in order to save my sister.

Put yourself in my position for a second, and see how your moral compass would point North when it was a family member's life at stake. You'd, like me, do anything to save an innocent fifteen-year-old girl from the hands of a gang that would, without guilt or remorse, use, rape or even kill her. There was nothing I wouldn't do to save Annie from the hell named the Night Skulls. Even if I had to help a ruthless mobster get the one girl he wanted so he'd give me the only person that mattered in my life.

"I'm not dating that monster!" She spun and braced against the sink, crying again. "What makes you think I'm that important to him he'll grant me that favor in exchange for one date anyway? Why don't you go ask Mona? He's taking her out tonight. Maybe *she* can help."

Her tone burned with jealousy, and I realized, again, my assumptions were wrong. Bianca wasn't afraid of Cosimo Lanza or didn't want to date him. She wanted him as much as he wanted her, and he was successful to make her jealous with his little stunt with Mona.

"Bianca," I chuckled, "he's not taking her out."

"Yes, he is. She just told me."

I rubbed her back gently, looking at her blubbering face in the mirror. "Trust me. I was there. I saw the whole thing. He was furious that you weren't there, and then he forced her to sit on his lap. Obviously, he told her to lie to you about that date to make you jealous. And it's working."

She lifted her head and stared at me, a hint of a smile curving the corner of her mouth. Then she glanced down, puckering her lips, and opened the faucet. "I'm not jealous. I don't care about that asshole or who he dates."

"Yeah, sure. That's why you were hiding in the kitchen all the time he was here, and all these tears are just from chopping onions there."

She splashed her face with water before she shrugged. "Fine. I might have gotten a little jealous when I thought he was taking Mona out."

"And you want to date him."

She was about to lie again, but I stared her down. She blew out a sigh. "He's the most dangerous man in town. I can't…like him."

But she did. It was written all over her face. Another antihero romance women swooned over. I got the appeal. Bad boys weren't afraid to go that extra mile to have you, keep you or save you. They'd make your dreams come true no matter what. It was great in fiction, but in reality, they were no antiheroes. They were the villains. I had no clue how girls fell that easily for real, bad, tattooed, dangerous boys. They did nothing but ruin lives, and the women they loved them always paid the price.

Bianca's dad was one of those. He ruined her mother's life with drugs and almost ruined Bianca's. If it weren't for Mr. Alfarez who took them in after her dad left, who knew what would have happened to them? Sylvia, too. She'd followed one bad boy after another, breaking Dad's heart, until she wound up a lonely, drunken bitch that had failed to even notice her daughter went missing for twenty-four hours.

A weak, pathetic excuse of a mother that had chosen the coward's way out instead of staying to help me find Annie or be there for me.

"Cameron, hey, don't cry, please," Bianca said.

I wasn't aware I was crying until I felt the tears drop on the back of my hand. I should never cry over Sylvia. Only Annie deserved my tears and concern and love.

Bianca held my arms. "Look, I'll do it."

My eyes widened at her as I snapped myself out of the hideous memories. "You will?"

"Yes. I'll help you, Cameron."

Tears flooded out of my eyes, tears of hope and gratitude, not pain. "Thank you so much. I will never forget this. If you want anything—"

"I want you to get Annie back. That's all that matters now."

"Thank you, Bianca. I'll always be in debt to you."

"Don't thank me yet. We still have one problem."

"What is it?"

"We have to get past Papi Carlos."

"Mr. Alfarez? Why?"

"He doesn't want me anywhere near Cosimo. He's been refusing Cosimo every time he asked to date me, stalling until I get my degree and leave the city. I owe him everything. I can't do this without his permission."

The hope that submerged me a minute ago flickered. "Okay. We'll go ask him. I think when he knows it's for Annie, he'll agree."

"Yes. Sure. I hope so."

CHAPTER 6

CAMERON

"Absolutely not." Carlos Alfarez shattered all my hopes with two words.

"It's just one date, Papi," Bianca said.

"It'll never be one date. Once you open the door for the devil, he'll never go away."

"Mr. Alfarez, I'm begging you." I was desperate. "The Lanzas are my only hope to get Annie back. They're the ones who can force the Night Skulls to return her to me."

He looked at me pensively. "You don't want any favors from the Lanzas. Trust me."

"I'm at that point of my life where I'm ready to sell my soul to the Devil himself if he'll get me Annie. Can you imagine the horrors she's subjected to every day, every second with those monsters? I'm the only one she has left. I'd be damned if I didn't do anything in my power to save and protect her."

"I understand, and you're welcome to give customers posters and ask them if they've seen her or if they have any information to help you. But that's all I can offer. I will never allow Bianca to date Cosimo, not once, not ever."

"But, Mr. Alfarez—"

"Now, *you* please try to understand I, too, have to protect my daughter. If you don't, I'm afraid you won't be welcome here anymore." He stood, not allowing Bianca or me to say another word, practically kicking me out of his tiny office at the diner.

"I'm so sorry, Cameron. I tried," Bianca said.

I nodded at her once. "It's not your fault. Thanks anyway." I collected my things and dashed out, anger bubbling up inside me. I stared at this city of pain where monsters like the Lanzas and the Night Skulls ruled with fear and malice. Where people like me and Annie were nothing but a form of entertainment for them, to take, use and abuse whenever they felt like, and we just had to submit and take whatever they dished out. Because they were rich and powerful and criminals and we were not.

Bent over in agony, I screamed out loud, saying my sister's name at the top of my lungs for everyone to hear it, tears bursting from my eyes. My sister was taken, and there was nothing I could do to bring her back.

No. I refused to give up. I refused to be one of the weak.

I straightened my back and glared at the diner. I couldn't blame Alfarez for trying to protect the girl he raised. In his way, he might have been protecting me, too. He wasn't my father, though. I was old enough to know what was best for me. It was my job to protect Annie, and I'd do it no matter what.

If Bianca wouldn't help, I'd go to the Lanzas myself.

I ran to the bank and got all the money I had left before they closed for the day. Then I went to Dad's house—where I'd been living since the abduction—to change.

Much to my surprise, Mr. Alfarez was waiting at the door. "We need to talk."

I let him in and offered him a beer. "If you're here to make sure I don't bother Bianca again about the Lanzas, don't worry. I'm going to deal with them myself."

The plan was simple. Go to Cosimo Lanza directly and offer him the money in exchange for bringing Annie back. He was still Mafia. If there was anything he wanted more than the girl, it was money. He'd never say no to money.

I didn't know where he lived or where he did business, but I knew he'd be at Alfarez tonight to pick up *Mona*. I'd make my proposal there, and Annie would be back home.

"I'm here to make sure you don't have anything to do with the Mob. You don't know how dangerous they are," he said.

"Thank you for your concern, Mr. Alfarez, but I'm old enough to make my own choices in life, and right now this is the right choice." The only choice.

He shook his head. "Listen, Cameron. I know you think it's the only way to save your sister, but what you're about to do isn't going to bring her back. You think the Lanzas are going to favor you for a few thousands over the Night Skulls that make them millions?"

"What?"

"They're friends, Cameron. The MC facilitates their drug and gun businesses. They won't lose them for your sake or even Bianca's. You can't afford to pay them off. And even if Cosimo takes your money and says yes, you have to know that he'll come back asking for more, and you'll never be able to say no. If you make any kind of connection with the Lanzas, it's for life. You can't get out."

I shook my head in despair. "I'll have to take that risk."

"But—"

"But what? Let Roar and his gang rape my little sister every fucking day for the rest of her life?" I clenched my jaws hard so I wouldn't cry.

"I didn't say that. I'm saying there's another way."

"What way? What else can I do?"

"Ever heard of the Belle View dance club?"

A dance club? Seriously? "Yes, but I've never been. Is there some other gang there that can bring my sister back but less evil that will let me get off with a one-time payment?"

He scoffed. "I don't want you to deal with any gang. I want you to take matters into your own hands so you won't be in debt to any son of a bitch out there."

I threw my hands in the air in frustration. "I can't stand up to the Night Skulls by myself."

"You won't have to. Just hear me out, kid. Since he returned home, Dusty has been spending every night in that club. All you have to do is get to that boy. He'll bring Annie back for you."

"Wait a minute, who's Dusty, and what does he have to do with my sister?" I asked impatiently.

He leaned back, taking a swig from the beer. "Dusty is Roar's boy."

"And that monster's son will help me get my sister his father kidnapped?"

"Not exactly, but I have a plan if you're willing to listen."

CHAPTER 7

DUSTY

Bodyguards in Italian suits crawled inside the Belle View, stiffening the air. I might have been out of Roar's lifestyle, the MC and its affiliations for the past couple of months, but I still recognized mobsters when I saw them.

I downed my beer as the Lanza twins entered and headed straight toward me. This was no random night out or a coincidence. They came here to meet me.

One of them—the capo, Cosimo, I guessed as I could never tell them apart— opened his arms, with a wide smile, as if I were his long-missed friend, and gave me a hug. "Dusty, welcome home."

I plastered a smile, too; his brother was watching me like a hawk. "Thanks. It's only been two months."

"Two months too long for a mother whose only son disappeared without a single phone call."

I broke the embrace, fighting not to roll my eyes. "So it's Mama who told you I was here?" The Lanzas and the Night Skulls were allies and had tons of business together. Mama and Roar were personal friends to Giovanni Lanza and Cosimo, his son, after he took over when Giovanni died. Did she reach out to the Lanzas to track me down and bring me back to Rosewood? After what happened that night, I swore I'd never go back. Not even the Mob could force me to return to that hell pit. "What else did she say?"

"C'mon, Dusty. There's nothing that happens in this city that we don't know."

"Not just this city," his brother, Enzio, said, resting his elbows on the bar top. "We heard about your little escapades in Europe. Looks like you enjoy it there since you only came home for one night two months ago and rushed back there. Are you planning to stay longer this time or heading back so soon?"

My eyes narrowed at them. I wasn't sure where this conversation was heading. "Looks like we're gonna have a long night. What can I get you, gentlemen? It's on me."

Cosimo took a seat next to mine and folded an arm around my shoulder. "Before we have a drink together, I wanna make sure you understand something. Our families go way back, Dusty. We don't want anything to disturb our friendship, right?"

I looked him in the eye, clenching my jaws instead of breaking his arm. This wasn't a friendly visit as I thought it'd be. This meet was set to intimidate me, but I wasn't sure why. "Yeah."

"Allora, I heard a little rumor that you had a falling-out with Roar. I get it, trust me. Fathers," he chuckled, "they have their moments. Mine and I didn't always see eye to eye, but at the end of the day, we were always, *always*, family."

"What's that got to do with me, Cosimo?"

"I'm sure it's just another little rumor that you left the MC."

Mama wouldn't have told him that. Was it Roar? He was the kind of father that wouldn't hesitate to send his mobster friends to straighten out his boy into falling back in line. But no, he was too arrogant to involve someone else in our fight. He'd have just sent some brothers. The Lanzas weren't only here as a favor to their friends. They were also here to protect their turf. "I don't see how that's any of your business, but you're right. It's just a fucking rumor," I lied. "I'm still wearing my cut, aren't I?"

"And that visit to your rival MC in Italy, the Wicked Warriors?" Enzio asked.

"I see what this is all about now." I shrugged Cosimo's arm off me and drank my beer. "I'm still a member of the Night Skulls." Even if I wanted nothing to do with them anymore. The tattoos on my body would never be inked out. They were my family after all. I'd never put them in any kind of danger. Loyalty went beyond code. "You think I left to prospect for another club, but I'm not. You can assure Roar and Mama I'm loyal."

"Then what were you doing with the Wicked?" Cosimo asked.

What I saw the night I decided to leave Rosewood and go back to Europe even when I'd just returned sent me on another quest to find answers to this life we led. I visited the Wicked Warriors to know if all MCs were the same. If it was Roar that was evil or the lifestyle itself that corrupted every member beyond retribution.

I couldn't tell them that, though. I couldn't tell them I only wore my cut so that the world would think I was still loyal to the Night Skulls. No one should know I left the MC two months ago and swore never to go back. I couldn't give any rival or the pigs any opportunity to think we were falling from within or that I, the heir to Roar's throne, disagreed with his ways.

I smiled at the brothers. "They throw crazy parties, and that was all I was about in Europe. I'm sure you heard of that, too." I took another swig from my beer. "And to give you even more peace of mind, I'm not planning on starting my own club or acting based on any of those shitty rumors you keep hearing. You and Roar can keep your turf. No one is setting to take it from you." I finished the beer. "I'm a Night Skull for life." Bitterness filled my throat with the reality I couldn't change. "I'm having another beer. Are you joining me or should we spend the rest of the night drinking Lanza wine at one of your fancy restaurants?"

Cosimo chuckled as he left his seat. "Another time. I had the restaurant booked for a private party for two, if you know what I mean. I'd better not be late."

Enzio followed him. "You're sure she's coming?"

"I ran out of patience. She doesn't have a choice anymore." Cosimo buttoned his suit jacket and patted my shoulder. "Dopo, Dusty. Ah, and call your mamma. She's worried sick about you."

CHAPTER 8

CAMERON

I didn't know what Mr. Alfarez was sniffing, but that plan was the craziest thing I'd ever heard. There was no way in hell I'd do any of the things he said I should do. I was sticking to *my* plan.

Just so he wouldn't try to stop me when I showed up tonight at the diner, I assured him I'd listen and wouldn't go seek the Lanzas' help. After I saw him out, I stuffed the money in my backpack, waited for evening to come and went straight to the diner. Strangely, there were more people scattered outside it than inside, and the door was blocked by two hulks in black suits.

"Walk away," one of them barked at me.

"I need to go in there." My sister's life depended on it. "I must see Mr. Lanza."

"I said walk away." He glared down at me, his tone menacing. "Don Lanza doesn't want to see anyone right now."

There was no doubt these two were Cosimo Lanza's bodyguards, and by the looks of it, he'd kicked everyone out of the diner. Fuck.

What was I supposed to do now? Why did every time I came up with a plan to save my sister something or someone shit on it?

I wasn't going to give up, though. I had to get in there.

Summoning my courage, I dared ask the bodyguard to move so I could go in and meet Cosimo. His gun answered me this time.

I stepped back, swallowing, but then I saw another gun. It was Cosimo's. Inside the diner, he'd just pulled out his gun, and Bianca was shaking, mumbling something at him. "What the fuck?" I looked around for help, but everybody was pretending not to see. "Can someone do something?!"

No one answered, their eyes begging me to act as if I saw nothing just like earlier when he was threatening Mona. That was bullshit. You couldn't just watch people you cared about get hurt and do nothing because it was the *safe* fucking choice.

She was my friend, and a very bad man pulled a gun on her, sending her to her knees, and everyone was turning a blind eye. Just like with Annie. They saw her on Roar's bike and no one lifted a finger to stop him from riding away with her.

I pulled out my phone. My first instinct was to call the cops, but I remembered how useless they were finding my sister. If they were in Roar's pocket, they were definitely on the Lanzas' payroll, too.

No, I wouldn't call the cops. I'd call Alfarez. He was right not to let Bianca date Cosimo, and I was wrong to even think about dragging her into a deal with the devil.

Before the call went through, Bianca was out of the diner with Cosimo, smiling, as he led her to his Mercedes. She gave me a brief glance that was void of the pleasure stretching her lips. Then when she spotted the phone in my hand, she shook her head once, before she was dragged to the car by the Mafia boss, the bodyguards surrounding them like hawks. Then the Mercedes cruised away.

Just like that, evil won again today.

CHAPTER 9

CAMERON

A noisy sound boomed over the muffled beat streaming from the Belle View dance club into the street.

Dusty's Harley.

The sound I'd been waiting to hear for hours. I didn't mind. I'd have waited for him to show up until the end of the night. And many nights to come. What were a few more days to eight months? Could you believe it'd been eight months since Annie was taken? Eight months of pain and fear and helplessness?

It was ridiculous how things panned out. I'd spent all my life trying to be a good person, a good student, a good daughter and sister. I'd done everything in my power to protect Annie, and she ended up taken by a notorious gang. Mr. Alfarez did the right thing and tried to protect Bianca for years, yet she ended up with Cosimo anyway. They were getting married for fuck's sake.

Mr. Alfarez was right about one thing, though. The Lanzas would have never helped me. They wouldn't take my money, and Cosimo Lanza wouldn't even grant his fiancée that one favor of helping her friend getting her abducted sister back. Business in millions turned out to be far more important than love or family or anything else for monsters like Cosimo and Roar.

I squeezed the steering wheel, eyes pinned to Dusty's small reflection in the rear mirror, one thought in my head. Tonight, I'd get what I came here for.

He pulled up in front of the club and killed the engine. The bouncer greeted him with a brotherly handshake, a hug, and a little chuckle.

Lucky for me, Dusty didn't fit the filthy biker stereotype that only went to MC bars to bang cheap whores and chug down beers for everyone to hear how loud he could belch.

Despite being the son of Roar, The Night Skulls' fucking President, Dusty drove his bike alone, without the gang flanking him, and went to uptown dance clubs in San Francisco. I'd been watching him for months and was sure he'd show up here alone. The perfect setting for my plan. Well, the plan I'd once ridiculed when Mr. Alfarez proposed it, which now I modified, improved and was ready to implement because all the doors had been closed in my face, and it was my last shot. Tonight I got my sister back or lost everything.

I waited for a few minutes after Dusty went inside the club, and then I followed. The next part was easy. All it took was a blond wig, a skanky mini dress and makeup, and skankier moves on the dance floor to get him buzzing around me like a fly drawn to an exposed honeypot.

He didn't recognize me. I didn't think he would. Not unless The Night Skulls handed every member a poster of my face with a warning below. The way they'd been behaving since Annie was officially a cold case, riding around town, not even trying to threaten me or shut me up, fucking offering to help with the search for the *missing girl*, said they were too arrogant to bother with me. I was too insignificant.

There was no such thing as being too careful, though. I learned that the hard way. The disguise I wore was to lure Dusty in, and for later, when the security guards or any friends of Dusty's here were asked to id the woman he was with all night, the new look would come in handy.

I did my best not to look like myself in case any of the few gang members who knew me showed up unannounced. They probably wouldn't have recognized me either with the wig and all the makeup. I didn't look like the Cameron they knew at all.

When I sat at the bar, Dusty offered to buy me a drink. I nodded, giving him a small—hopefully sexy—smile. I didn't speak, afraid my voice would shake or give him any hint of the psyche underneath. Even though I'd been planning this for months, determined to go through with it no matter what, I was nervous as fuck.

"What's your poison?" he asked, his hand— huge hand—around his beer.

I glanced at him. It was the first time I took a close look at his face. The dance floor was too dark to notice the details, and before tonight I'd always watched him from a distance.

The first thing that grabbed my attention was his smile. The kind that melted hearts and messed with heads. A very powerful weapon coming from those fleshy lips. His eyes weren't any less dangerous. Warm. Beautiful. Bright with shades of green in them.

He had thick, black hair that reached below his ear, a heavy stubble, and ink covering his neck. The white T-shirt and leather jacket must have hidden more tattoos…and muscles. Big ones. Lots of them. I could see the outline of his bench and six packs through his T-shirt. According to my information, he wasn't over twenty years old, but he looked more…masculine.

To say Dusty was good-looking was an understatement. He was really beautiful and didn't look anything like Roar. His piece of shit father was blond with long, unkempt hair. Rough face. Hard jaws. Sickening smile. He was large and rugged with a threatening presence—Dusty was large, too, but in a…more appealing way.

My gaze shifted to the barkeep. I wouldn't let myself be fooled by appearances. Even when everybody was saying Dusty wasn't a monster like his father, and I knew for sure he wasn't there when Annie was taken, he was still the son of the fucker that took my sister. He wore the Night Skulls' cut. He was one of them. "Whatever you're having."

Dusty ordered tequila shots and a beer. I had one shot with him so it wouldn't be too suspicious. I needed my strength and clarity tonight. He took a swig from the beer, and I fumbled with my purse and let it slip out of my hands. He put the bottle down and picked the purse off the floor for me.

"Thank you. I think I'm already tipsy." I pretended to giggle.

A crooked smile curved the corner of his mouth. "What do you say? Wanna get outta here?"

Goosebumps spread across my skin. "Okay. You finish your beer. I'll hit the lady's room real quick and meet you back here?"

He took another swig. "Sure, babe."

The second I hit the restroom, I braced myself against the sink, shutting my eyes, evening my breaths. *You can do this. It's all working according to plan. You can do this!*

As I opened my eyes, I noticed the few girls who were already inside. They were looking at me through the mirrors on the wall. "You all right?" One of them paused reapplying her lipstick to ask.

I stared at her for a moment, clutching at the marble to hide the shaking of my hands. Of course she didn't know when I dropped my purse earlier, I'd slipped a drug into Dusty's beer, and now I had to wait here for a few minutes before it kicked in. But my face must have shown how nervous and scared I was.

I never had second thoughts about what I was about to do to Roar's son. It didn't mean I was okay with it, though. I felt horrible. Torn. Afraid. How did those thugs from The Night Skulls do it with smirks on their faces? Taking someone, hurting them without an ounce of guilt or fear?

HOW?

The concerned look in the girl's eyes nudged me back to reality. Even remorse was a luxury I couldn't have. Nodding once at her, I wet my lips in silence. I spun and sprinkled some water on my face. Then I fixed my makeup and headed out.

No turning back now.

Dusty was still at the bar, finishing the last of his beer. I took a deep breath as I reached him. "Ready when you are."

He slid his arm around my waist, no signs of the drug on him yet, his hand low on my hip. Pictures of me breaking that hand to the point of permanent damage occupied my imagination all the way out of the club and to the parking lot.

The shiny Harley stood out in the middle of the lot, and he wanted to take me for a ride and then to his place.

Shit.

I needed him in my car. At my place. I laughed to hide my nerves. "You don't look like you have an extra helmet."

"You always follow the rules?" he retorted, fully sober.

Why the fuck was he not out yet? Did I mess up the dose? Or did he pretend to drink that beer? Oh my God, what if he figured it out or saw me slipping that drug?

My heart thrashed. *Don't freak out now. Just don't.*

I blinked, laughing under my breath, leaning into his chest. "How about we break some rules in the backseat of my car?"

His hands found my butt. "I like the way you think."

Quickly, I took his hands off my body and into my own palms, dragging him to the car. As soon as I unlocked it and opened the door, he pushed me inside and ducked in, slamming the door behind him.

"What the fuck?" I yelped, my eyes wide, curling heat sinking in my stomach.

His dangerous eyes washed over my body and then lifted to my face. The way he looked at me held me in place. Not out of fear. His gaze was rather warm and…sweet. That was never a word I thought I'd use to describe my enemy's son.

The back of his fingers brushed over my naked arm so softly. "Easy, kitty. I'm just messing with you. Didn't mean to scare you. Thought maybe you liked it a little rough, breaking the rules and all." He gave me that smile again and leaned in for a kiss.

"I don't," I breathed.

"That's a first."

"What do you mean?"

"All the girls I've met like to be dominated or even roughed out."

"Is that what *you* like?"

"When the girl is into it, yes. It's hot. But it's okay." His huge—wow—warm palm caressed half of my face with one stroke. "I can be sweet and gentle for you, baby. It's refreshing." He leaned in, his eyes dropping to my lips. I ran out of ideas or excuses to stall him, so I let him kiss me.

Damn. He really was sweet and gentle. He was making this so fucking hard. *Please pass out already.*

His lips grew greedy. Hungry. His hands too. Fuck. I couldn't take another second of this or him touching me. I almost vomited in his mouth and blew up the whole plan. Had we been different people at a different time, I wouldn't have minded the touching. I would have loved it, encouraged it with hungrier moves. He was beyond sexy. Any woman could fall into his arms without a second thought or regret. And the way he kissed me, the way his hands explored my body—despite everything—set me ablaze.

But we were not different people at a different time. I was Cameron, Annie's sister. He was Dusty, the son of her abductor.

I stopped his hands before they roamed any farther, ready to knock him out with force if I had to.

He cocked a brow at me suspiciously all of a sudden. "Wait... Something is... I..."

I stared at him, holding my breath, his eyelids drooping. Then his body went limp, and he was out.

Just like that. Eight months of agony and rage and waiting and planning reduced to the minutes it took Dusty to lose consciousness. A few minutes that felt like a fucking lifetime.

Now, let my revenge begin.

CHAPTER 10

DUSTY

Opening my eyes was not an easy task with the worst hangover headache ever splitting my skull in half.

Something wasn't right. I didn't get hangovers. How much did I drink last night anyway? Was that even a new day? It was pitch black in here.

Where the fuck am I? And why am I so fucking sore?

A chime of metal echoed when I tried to move. That was when I realized my arms were fucking shackled. My heart picked up as I kicked my feet, but I could only wiggle my toes. The sharp, cold restrains around my ankles held me in place.

"What the fuck is going on?!" I snapped at the chains, but I couldn't break loose. The burning in my arm muscles told me I'd been held aloft for hours on end.

When did that happen? I couldn't remember shit. I left the club with that chick and got into her car. We were making out, and then everything got fuzzy.

"Whoever did this is gonna pay!" I shouted, sweeping this lifeless place with my eyes, waiting for someone to answer. "Bad."

Dead silence.

I had another go at the shackles. It got me nowhere. Shaking my legs didn't work either. The resistance came from below, which meant the chains had been secured directly into the floor. My limbs were spread apart, rendering me immobile. Sweat broke along my forehead, and a cold shiver took over me. Fuck, I'd been naked all along.

I took a deep breath. Something reeked. Vomit maybe. A fresh wave of nausea brought a wet cough and a bad taste in my mouth. Maybe I did get hammered and threw up. Maybe I wasn't taken, and all this was a sick, sex game that chick liked to play.

"So you *do* like to play rough, huh?" I laughed. "Old school shackles and all. Okay. I like your style…Mistress…or whatever you like to be called." My eyes strained against the darkness to check for cameras, but I couldn't make out anything. She must have been watching, though. "You gonna come out and play now?"

All I heard back was the echo of my voice. Should I be relieved she wasn't there?

"Okay, this isn't funny anymore. I'm serious now. Come out and tell me what the fuck you want." Did that bitch come off to this shit? Watching naked men tied up?

More silence and that fucking smell filled the area.

"You know…I really liked you, but now you're just a bitch pissing me off." My body jerked, rattling all of my chains at once. "If you don't come out now, I swear I'm gonna kill you myself."

My arms and legs hurt more with every violent move I made to free myself. There was no way to tell how much more time had passed while I froze in this shithole. Seconds. Minutes. But it sure felt like forever.

Why would some cute blond chick pull something like that? With someone like me? She knew who I was. The bike and the cut couldn't be missed. Did she think she was gonna get away with it? The Night Skulls took no prisoners. Well, they took some for pleasure but never one who had crossed them.

I had to consider the possibility she just didn't care. The first thought that came to my head that if she wasn't threatened by my notorious family, maybe she came from one as fucked up as mine.

Gang rivalry? Some payback? Settling score with my shitty-ass dad? What was it she wanted from me? What would she do when she was…finished? A girl kidnapping a man like me must have been capable of much more. Was she a killer?

Something rumbled and screeched. Then the first ray of light I'd seen since I woke up flared in my eyes. The next second, I heard a thud, and the light vanished, immediately replaced by a stronger glare. A flashlight, I guessed.

A form approached, but I couldn't make out whose it was. The small steps, however, told me it was a woman. It must have been her.

"Hey! You'd better set me loose now. What the fuck is this shit you think you're doing?"

She didn't answer. The sound of her steps did the talking. They weren't cautious or hesitant but firm. I knew for sure now that girl wasn't playing. She took me on purpose, and the consequences didn't scare her.

My eyes hardly adjusted to the new light, but I could see her now. She looked so much different. Brunette with a clean face. More mature. Like a woman not a girl. Was she even the same chick I met? "What the fuck is going on? Who the hell are you?"

She moved, and the light moved with her. Metallic noises screeched in my ears. Then the light returned to glare in my face. She was sitting in front of me now, the flashlight on the cement floor. Those noises must have been her grabbing that chair where she sat. "My name is Cameron."

The voice was the same. I remembered because she had that rasp that I thought was so damn hot. "Fuckever. Take this shit off me." I rocked my arms. "Now."

"What? You don't like my style anymore?" she taunted.

I did.

I was in pain, pissed, shackled and fucking naked in front of this bitch—who for some wicked reason was so much hotter now with dark hair, tank top and jeans—but I'd never felt so much...thrilled.

There was something excitingly dangerous about being under a woman's command. A new feeling that shot my adrenaline to the roof. And every time she spoke with that rasp, despite the freezing cold and this fucked up mess, my cock sprang to life.

Shit. She could fucking see.

An angry chuckle burst out of my mouth. "I'm done playing, *Cameron*. You'd better end this right now. Maybe, just maybe, there's a one percent chance you won't wind up fucked to death."

She stood from her chair and stepped toward me, her expression unreadable. Her head lifted so she could look me in the eyes. "Is that so?"

I leveled my gaze with hers, smirking. "Yeah. I'd take you for myself instead."

Oh I wanted to fuck her. I wanted to fuck her so hard. Many times.

Something hell-like flicked in her eyes. "You and your fucking gang like to take girls for yourselves all the time, don't you?! Rip them from their families and keep them around to fuck all you want?" She was yelling, but her voice cracked at the end.

My mind raced with thoughts and horrible memories the family I was born into had given me. The Night Skulls were outlaws who had committed many crimes including the abduction of young girls. The heat in this woman's breath and the intensity of her emotions revealed what could be the reason she was holding me here.

The Night Skulls had kidnapped one of her own.

"What are you talking about?" I played dumb.

Her jaws tightened, the gritting of her teeth audible. She reached inside the pocket of her jeans and brought a folded piece of paper. When she unfolded it, she shoved it in my face.

For a second, as I saw who that photo belonged to, I froze.

Her eyes sparkled. "You know her?" It was more of a revelation than a question.

The pain searing through my body increased. Tenfold. "Never seen her before," I lied to her face, snatching my stare away from the picture.

"Don't you dare lie to me," she said through her teeth.

I had to. What else would I tell her? That my father kidnapped her? That this innocent kid was…

I couldn't finish the thought. I just looked away.

"Listen, Dusty, I know you were out of town when Roar took her, but I also know you returned a few days later. You must have seen her with him…or with any of the gang." Her eyes pleaded at me almost in tears. "Just tell me. What happened to my sister?"

"How did you know any of that?"

"The same way I know your real name is Dustin Bowell. And you'd be at the Belle View when I met you," she replied. "I've been watching you and your fucking pieces of shit of a family since the day the police stopped looking for Annie and tried to convince me she ran away and never was kidnapped."

Fuck. "Look I'm sorry for what you've been through, but you're wrong. I have never seen your sister, and my…father and the club has nothing to do with her either."

She took a deep breath and leaned closer, studying my face. The silence was excruciating, but I hid everything I felt behind years of practice. I might have been a Night Skull just to keep pretenses and not at heart, but I never forgot what they taught me. They had trained me well.

"I thought you were smarter than that," she finally said.

I glared at her. "You don't know who you're dealing with. If you don't let me go now, they'll find you, and they'll hurt you, in ways you could never imagine."

Cameron stepped back, folding her arms across her chest. "I don't doubt they'll come for me. Actually, I'm counting on it."

CHAPTER 11

CAMERON

"From what I see you have two choices, Dusty. One, you tell me about my sister, help me get her back, and no one is harmed. Two, I beat the crap out of you until you tell me everything, and I'll go save my sister on my own."

He laughed. He fucking laughed. "You? Will beat the crap out of me?"

I kicked him straight in the nuts.

"Motherfucker!" he howled, his limbs tense, the sinews bulging.

Without giving him time to recover, I punched him in the gut. His abs were so firm they almost fractured my knuckles.

Fuck, he was too damn distracting with all that muscle perfection, as if he was cut out from a fucking magazine. The huge thing with fucking rings dangling between his legs was another story. Much to my dismay, I could swear I saw it semi-hard at a moment or two, but it was probably my mind playing tricks on me.

Who would get hard in such situation? Kidnapped, helpless and humiliated like this?

I knew girls went crazy over these situations in books, but I never read about a man who would…or a girl on the other side, the one with the power to do whatever she wanted to her captive.

I had to admit, I'd crossed my arms over my chest so he wouldn't see how hard my nipples had become when I stood close to him. It wasn't just because he was naked. The ability to do anything to him while he couldn't lift a finger was…more than arousing. Something twisted I never thought I'd feel. A side I didn't know I had until now. Maybe that man who liked being dominant and rough had a different side, too, and what I thought I saw was true.

Unless…

Unless he didn't feel helpless or humiliated in the first place.

He growled in pain. "Fuck you, bitch."

A surge of anger coursed through me. I tore my eyes from his naked body. If I was going to threaten him and mean it, I needed my focus. My anger that would never fade until I found my sister.

I grabbed on the rage like a shield when my eyes returned on him. My fists balled again ready for another swing.

"All right. All right! You proved your point," he said, his breaths labored. "God, you're strong."

For the past six months, I'd been working out like crazy, taking self-defense classes, even learning how to shoot. For this moment. "Where's my sister?"

"I don't know."

My palm found his cheek this time. His head whipped to the side, then jerked back at me, his eyes defiant, wild.

It stirred something in me I couldn't control. Something as defiant and wild as his gaze. Something equally dangerous.

A smirk tightened his murderous gaze. "You like that, don't you? I bet you're fucking dripping right now."

"Fuck you." I hated him because he was right. He could see right through the inexplicable attraction swirling through me.

"With pleasure. Unchain me, and I'll show you what a good fucking is. You look like you need it…bitch."

My jaws clenched. "If you think you're protected by your scumbags, you're wrong. Even when they come for me, they can't save you because they will never find you. I've been planning this, building this place, for months for that purpose alone." I looked him straight in the eye. "You'd better start talking, asshole."

He stared at me, his expression a question mark. His lips parted as if he was going to say something, but his chin lowered, and his eyes found the floor.

I followed the path his gaze took and clashed with the enormous erection he was sporting. I swallowed. Up close, he had so many rings in it and a tattoo. Who the hell tattooed their own cock?

"Like what you see? Maybe you wanna give me a hand…or a mouth. I'm not picky."

"You're sick."

He chuckled. "Says the bitch that drugged and kidnapped me and now she's staring at my cock while she's shackling me in a fucking dungeon. Be honest, kitty. How wet are you right now?"

I slapped him again. "What the fuck did you do to Annie?"

Sweat splattered in the air when he jerked his head, his hair longer now that it was wet. "Nothing! Fucking nothing!" He curled his upper lip under his teeth and closed his eyes for a second. "I don't know where your fucking sister is. Assuming the Night Skulls took her, you said it yourself. I wasn't there when it happened."

"That was eight months ago. You must have seen her when you came back."

"Haven't you been watching me? You didn't notice that I hadn't been living in Rosewood since I returned?"

"What are you trying to make me believe? That you have nothing to do with her abduction? I know that, but that doesn't make you innocent. You lived in Rosewood when she was taken. You recognized her picture. You fucking saw her. So why don't you save us both some time and tell me where they're keeping her?"

"If it's really info you're looking for, you're wasting your time. You've got the wrong guy. I can't help you because…" a deep line appeared between his brows, "…I left the MC."

"What? That's impossible. You're lying. You still wear the cut and drive the bike." I gazed at the tattoos on his neck, chest and arms. Skulls and roses. The Night Skulls' emblem. "You have their fucking tattoos all over you."

"Can't exactly let people know the prince has left the castle, can I? The family has a reputation to keep." He blew out a long breath. "But something tells me this is not news to you."

It was. If anything, I suspected he had fallen out with them, but I never thought he'd left. That was his family, not just a gang he joined. "Why the fuck are you lying to me?"

"I'm not."

"If that was the truth, why would you tell me? To feel sorry for you? To make me feel guilty for capturing the saint of the Night Skulls and set you free?"

"No. I'm no fucking saint. I'm telling you because it feels good to say it. I'm telling you because if there's any chance it'll change your mind about your stupid plan, it'll be worth it." He held my gaze, his eyes bright and warm and mesmerizing. "You're not a criminal, Cameron. I can tell. You're a good girl."

"Fuck you."

A shadow of defeat dimmed his gaze. "You didn't take me to tell you where your sister is. You knew I wouldn't talk, Night Skull or not. I'd never betray my family."

Quick. I'd give him that. I didn't kidnap him to chat. Whether he was with the gang or not wouldn't make any difference. I didn't hold him here because he was a Night Skull. He was my captive because he was Roar's only son.

"You're planning on a trade," he concluded.

Yes. That was how he'd help get her back.

He looked at me for a long moment with… I didn't know what that was. Not blame or anger or menace. Something else entirely different with the same warmness I felt when he kissed me, and it set me spiraling with guilt. "Don't let them drag you down with them. You still have a soul. Don't let them taint it. There's no going back from there."

My eyes burned with unshed tears. I turned my back to him. I couldn't let him see any softness in me. Any weakness. However, I wanted to burst into tears. I wanted to beg him to forgive me. What I did was wrong. Ugly. Like what they did to Annie.

"Thank you so much for your fucking concern with my soul. How caring of you! Did you do the same for Annie, too?"

"Cameron—"

"Shut the fuck up." I had to silence him. There was no room for remorse or guilt. The good in me had to be smothered by the darkness I needed to bear to deal with those monsters.

Dusty might have had nothing to do with Annie's abduction. He might not have been a

Night Skull anymore. But once a Night Skull always a Night Skull. I had to tell myself that to justify what I'd done. What I was about to do.

I had no choice but to go with my plan even if I was going to hell for it. He was my leverage. My only hope to get Annie back.

His life for hers.

CHAPTER 12

DUSTY

Cameron left me in the dark. To the cold. To the
pain numbing my body on the outside and eating
my soul on the inside.

Yes, I did have one. A soul. Burdened by the
crimes of Roar. A motherfucking load I carried
wherever I went.

As time passed in this shit hole, my body
wasn't the only thing breaking. I was unable to
move, but my mind was racing. I had no choice
but to come face to face with the truth I never
wished to accept.

Annie.

Fifteen. Brunette like her sister. Taken last year. By my own father. Cameron probably knew all that. What she didn't know was that her sister was taken as a welcome back home gift.

For me.

I cringed at the memory, but it wouldn't quit playing in my head. A horror movie on repeat. I'd returned from Europe after a couple of months visiting the spreading Night Skulls' chapters across the continent.

I returned to Rosewood, the massive estate where the Night Skulls lived and did business— my home for the first eighteen years of my life— with a different mind. The decision to ignore everything that bothered me, pretend it didn't exist, wasn't difficult anymore.

They threw me an over the top welcome home party full of all kinds of sinful pleasures. I was dazzled. Hypnotized. High on power. Dad was right. I was meant to live a certain life. The time had come for me to accept it. The life of royalty. The whole world was under my feet.

He'd almost won me over. Almost.

I'd never forget the triumphant smile on his face after the party when he brought a little girl to my room. One special gift saved for last for me to unwrap.

She was shaking, her brown eyes big with fear. One look at them and everything changed.

Her feet barely moved toward me. Roar grabbed her by the hand and pulled her to my bed. Then he bragged about how he snatched her in the middle of the day, thinking she would be the best gift to give me.

Just because he could. And he thought I'd enjoy it as much as he did.

"You like brunettes more than blondes, right? She's a virgin, too. I checked her myself." He'd cracked a laugh as tears had streamed down her face. "C'mon. Stop whining, bitch." He'd smacked her with the back of his hand, sending her tumbling on her back.

"Dad!" The only word I'd managed to say.

Another laugh, more like a snort. "Whatever. Enjoy your night." He'd staggered out of the room, and I'd hurled until my stomach hurt.

The sound of her sobbing and the pleading look in her eyes wouldn't be erased from my memory until the day I died.

Fucking a chick who wanted to be fucked, even if it was rough, was cool. I didn't mind having as many of those as I could. Forcing my cock inside one, let alone a fifteen-year-old, was fucked up. Rape was beyond sick. To me. To Roar and pretty much every guy in the club, it was the norm. Annie was just another piece of meat. Fresh pussy to fuck.

"I won't touch you," I'd finally said.

She'd remained speechless, curled up on my bed. She wasn't feisty like her sister. No fire in her soul. Broken. Was she a helpless little girl before he took her? Or did he break her in the few days he had her in before I arrived?

I didn't stick long enough to find out. That night I took off and vowed to leave the Night Skulls for good.

I should have taken her with me, though. I should have listened to her pleas and saved her ass like I'd saved mine.

"Please, get me out of here. I beg you. I won't tell anyone. I'd tell my family I ran away with some guy. Please don't leave me here with him." She'd knelt on the floor and grabbed on my ankle like I'd been her only hope in this life.

She must have thought I was naïve or weak for not fucking her, and she could have used me to save her ass. That was what I'd told myself; she couldn't have meant what she'd said; she couldn't have been too terrified to say anything about the club.

The truth was I was more of a Night Skull than I thought I'd been. I'd cared more about my family than I'd cared about that girl and what could have happened to her.

She must be working the bars now or sold around like the other bitches Roar owned.

Maybe, he took her for himself. Maybe, she was even dead.

All because I'd kicked her off me that night and never looked back.

The reason behind Annie's abduction, the asshole that had left her to rot in hell, was shackled in her sister's basement or whatever dump this was, and Cameron had no clue.

CHAPTER 13

DUSTY

It was impossible to tell the time here, which drove me insane. I couldn't stand all those hours in the dark, freezing to death, alone. With my demons.

If I couldn't tell what day it was, I'd make up my own timeline. By how famished and thirsty and needing to piss I was, I'd decided when she was here, it was morning. The first morning after she'd kidnapped me. Now it was night. And she never showed up.

The bitch wasn't torturing me with her hands. She'd left me to torment myself. As if she knew what I'd done.

"How long are you gonna leave me like this?" I yelled at the emptiness, writhing in the fucking chains. My wrists and ankles scorched me as if they were being cut off.

I swore and screamed my lungs out in vain. The pain was hard enough not to let me sleep. I twisted violently against the shackles, causing more pain, hoping it'd knock me out.

The first attempt was a total bust. The second. The third. Each one felt like I was going to lose a limb. By the time I reached the eighth trial, my mind and body finally switched off.

Not for long.

A sweet smell awakened my senses, a warm breath on my face sending a shiver down my spine. I blinked and saw a blur of Cameron. My eyes snapped open, and she was staring at me with her big brown ones.

"How could you sleep?" The rasp was huskier than usual. She just woke up or hadn't been getting any sleep herself?

She was standing too close. If she'd been my height, I could have banged my head against hers, breaking her skull, giving her a concussion that wouldn't heal. Or...

I could have crushed my lips into hers.

I preferred the latter.

Mouth too dry to swallow, I glanced down. Shit. Wrong move. I stood a few inches higher, and I could see her tits down the V neck of her green sweatshirt.

Suddenly, she flinched, stumbling back a step with a glare. I didn't know the reason behind her panic until her stare dipped and I followed the destination it'd just reached. Oh fuck.

"What the hell is wrong with you?" she shouted, her eyes wandering between my face and my dick that was poking her a second ago.

"Spare me the fucking judgment. You were dripping the last time I was hard so cut the act. This time, it's not what you think anyway. I need to take a piss," I lied. I did need to piss, but that wasn't the only reason behind that motherfucking hard-on.

She looked at me as if she'd smelled something disgusting. Then she vanished in the dark, some rummaging sounds in the background. When she emerged in the light range, she had a plastic bottle in her hand.

I arched a brow. "Really?"

She approached, her gaze avoiding mine. "It's either this or you piss yourself."

"You know you're gonna have to hold it for me?" I couldn't help the smile tugging at my lips.

"I'm not going to hold your fucking cock."

The smile turned into a grin. "I didn't tell you to hold it. I meant the bottle. See who's aching to touch who, babe? It's okay. Don't be shy. If you wanna hold my co—"

She shoved the bottleneck tight around me, silencing me. I growled. "That fucking hurt."

"Good."

My piss trickled inside the plastic until it filled half the bottle. She took it off me gently this time. A drop or two glistened from my dick and onto the cement. "What if I need to take a dump?"

"You need to eat for that. Do you see me feeding you?"

My stomach snarled as if on cue. "Can I have some water, at least?"

She pushed the bottle in the little space between us, bringing it closer to my mouth.

"The fuck? I'm not gonna drink my own piss, you bitch."

"Keep calling me that, and I'll force it down your throat."

Curses flashed inside my head, twitching my mouth, almost making their way out. My chest rose and fell with rage as I had to swallow them. How the fuck did I wind up in this crappy shit? A little bitch I could squash with one squeeze of my hand held me captive, threatening to make me drink my piss?

"Where are they keeping my sister, Dusty?"

"Why do you care? Just arrange for the trade, and if they have her, they'll bring her to you."

"What if they decide to screw me up or trick me? I can't trust the Night Skulls even when I have their precious prince in my grasp. I need a backup plan. I gotta know where my sister is to take her by force if I have to. So tell me? Where are they keeping her? It's not the bars or the strip clubs. I checked."

I stared at the cold darkness ahead of me. "I don't know anything about your sister."

"Tell me what happened to her, and I'll give you that water."

"I don't fucking know!"

She placed the bottle on the floor. Her steps hurried to the door.

"Hey! Where are you going?" I snapped, the metal shaking with me.

The door slammed in my ear. "Fuck this shit."

Don't leave me just like this, you bitch. I can't take this shit anymore.

I screamed in despair. Who knew how long she was going to leave me alone this time? "I'm gonna fucking kill you!"

In my rage, a new fear crept underneath, baffling and stupid. What if Roar and the brothers got to her before she came back? I should want that to happen, but I found myself worried instead. I didn't want them to find her. I knew the shit they'd do to her, and instead of welcoming it, it made me sick.

I convinced myself it was only because there was a possibility she wasn't lying when she said they wouldn't find me even when they caught her. And because I wanted *me* to have my revenge on her, not anyone else. But, deep down, the truth was just the idea of anyone's hand on her had me aching for carnage.

What the fuck was happening to me? I was edgy and not thinking straight. This imprisonment shit was getting to me. All the guilt I felt for this girl and her sister didn't help either. I couldn't think that way. I had to find a way to get out of here.

"Fuck you, Cameron." My clouded mind ran in circles, but it settled down when my gaze landed on the flashlight. She didn't take it with her, which only meant she'd come back.

My heart jumped at the noisy screech of the door. Her steps were heavier, angrier. In the spotlight, I saw a duffle bag in one hand and a small bottle of water in the other. I grew thirstier by the second, eyeing the transparent bottle, my tongue dry as a rock.

She dropped the bag next to the piss bottle. "The bag or the water?"

I frowned. "What's in the fucking bag?"

"You don't want to know." She bent and set the water bottle in by her foot. "But I'll show you anyway." The zipper squeaked under her fingers. Then she spread the opening, revealing the contents.

"What the fuck?"

CHAPTER 14

CAMERON

Whips. Electric shockers. Gags. Chokers. CBT devices I didn't know how to use—I didn't even know what CBT was till Chelsea explained it to me. The term alone, cock and ball torture, made me cringe.

I wasn't into any kinky stuff. Vanilla sex was all I knew, and by how fast my ex-boyfriends broke up with me, I'd say I wasn't pretty good at it.

After my last breakup, Chelsea had brought me this bag of toys, hoping I'd try new things, spice it up a little, but I'd gotten the call from

Sylvia about Annie's abduction. Needless to say the bag lay in my basement for eight months untouched.

I glanced up from it. For the first time ever, I saw fear in Dusty's eyes. The way he looked at the torturing tools peeking from the bag assured me he was no longer taking his situation lightly. He finally knew I wasn't goofing around, and I would use these tools without hesitation.

He was scared. Of me.

It turned me on like hell. I was soaking my panties by just looking at the fear on his face. What the fuck was wrong with me?

"What are you gonna do with these?" he whispered.

I rose to my feet, grabbing the water bottle. "If you tell me what happened to Annie, I won't do anything." I twisted the cap open. "And will give you some water."

"Why don't you believe me? I don't know your sister or what happened to her," he insisted, frustrated.

He was more than convincing, but my mind wouldn't ignore the way he looked at Annie's picture. "You fucking knew her." I threw the bottle in his face. The water splashed all over him. The bottle hit him in the chest then landed at his feet with strumming thuds against the cement.

He stuck out his tongue, licking all the droplets he could reach off his face. My sex clenched against my will.

Angry at myself before him, I grabbed the first item I could get from the bag and darted toward him.

"No. No! You don't wanna do this," he urged.

His words fell blank on my ears. When I reached him, I realized I was holding a whip with multiple tails. I swung it at his body. His incredible, bulging-with-muscle figure.

"Cameron, stop!"

I whipped him again without aim. That thing moved so fast I couldn't see where it was hitting him. "Where's Roar keeping Annie? What did he do to her?"

He squirmed and groaned, his hair ruffling, but he kept his lips sealed.

My strokes grew faster. Heavier. He didn't utter a word. Fury blazed inside me, and for some reason shifted to my core. I was possessed by a demon that got off to whipping a strong, bound man. "Goddamn it, just tell me!" I snapped.

Nothing.

I aimed at his penis this time. If that didn't make him talk...

The whip missed him the first time. It barely touched his balls, but it was hard enough to force some nasty swears out of his mouth. I didn't miss the second time. Or the third.

His wild groans were the sexiest sounds I'd ever heard. That was scary to admit, but I fucking liked what I was doing to him.

On the fifth, he lost control and quivered. His whole body, gleaming with sweat and water, shook against the restraints.

The sight of a strong man like Dusty, one that was capable of so much damage and violence, trembling in front of me, because of me and what I was doing to him triggered something in me. Something that squeezed my heart rather than cool the fire inside it.

I wouldn't lie about the twisted pleasure and arousal I discovered with these acts, but none of this was consensual. How low had I stooped? Was I that evil to torture a man, whip his genitals, send him shaking like this?

Finding my sister was the most important thing to me, but what if Dusty never spoke? How far would I go to extract the truth out of him?

I was certain his gang did a lot worse to Annie than what I did to him. Still, I didn't take him for revenge. It wasn't an eye for an eye thing. I only wanted to get my sister back.

The whip dropped from my fist, and, without thinking, I found myself wrapping my arms around his waist so tightly, rubbing his back to make him stop shuddering.

Weak. Pathetic. Stupid. Let him say whatever he wanted about me. I didn't care.

His tense muscles relaxed in my grip. Slowly, the tremors slowed. He rested his chin on my head, and when the shaking stopped, he kissed my hair.

Now, I was the one who was trembling. Pulling away, I dragged my gaze to his. "What did you do that for?"

"I'm sorry," he murmured.

"What do you mean you're sorry? You kissed my head." I stared at the red marks all over his chest and abdomen. "I just whipped you, and you kissed my fucking head."

"You just *hugged* me."

Yes. And it felt so damn good. I swallowed, groping for a believable lie to tell. "To stop all that shaking. I thought you were going to pass out, and I need you awake."

A tired smile crossed his face.

I stepped back, looking down. His huge erection stared back at me. I was too occupied with guilt that I failed to feel this monster against my stomach while I hugged him. "I can't believe you right now."

His head lulled back. "If it bothers you this much, you should put some clothes on me."

"Or maybe I should chop it off."

"You need me in one piece for the trade," he retorted.

Damn. He was right. I grumbled. "Why the hell do you keep getting hard, you asshole?"

"'Cause all this shit you're pulling is driving me nuts. It hurts like fuck, and I hate you for it, but… I don't know." He shook his head. "I can't stop thinking about kissing you."

CHAPTER 15

DUSTY

When she opened that bag, I remembered all the times I used similar toys on girls. How they drove them crazy, sending them so willing and soaking in submission. Not once had I thought the roles would be reversed and some bitch would use them on me. Without even my permission.

Not once had I thought I'd have fucking enjoyed it.

I'd never known that physical pain could make my cock hard and stiff as a fucking maypole, but it wasn't just the pain that sent me aching. It was the loss of all control to this badass woman that wasn't afraid to cross boundaries and get her hands dirty to protect her own, even when I didn't allow her to take it. It was even better.

Forced submission. Bitches went crazy for it in Europe. It wasn't my thing as I'd seen it so many times before at the club but not for mutual pleasure. It was how the brothers sold pussy around without getting so much of an objection or a protest from the bitches.

Cameron wasn't doing it for pleasure either, and I was no one's bitch. I wasn't submissive, and I doubted she knew she had a dominant side in bed. Maybe that was why, even when I should hate Cameron, my body loved what she was doing to me. Forcing me submit to *her*. Making me take pain for *her*. *Only* her. Or maybe it was the guilt I couldn't shake off. The punishment I knew I deserved for letting that innocent little girl suffer.

Then she had to crack and fucking hug me. Right there, she killed me. The whip didn't hurt as much as her embrace. It swallowed me whole and sealed her destiny in the darkness that brought us together, even if she didn't know it yet.

I might hate Cameron for taking me and reminding me of the guilt that was tearing me apart, I'd make her pay for what she'd done, but, now, after I trembled for her, after I felt her tenderness folding around me, I would never let her go.

Filling my nostrils with the scent of her hair, I kissed it. In my head, I was waiting for the moment when I'd kiss her lips and every inch of her body until she was shuddering harder than how she was quivering now by my little kiss on the top of her head.

Pulling away, she dragged her big brown eyes up to mine. "What did you do that for?"

"I'm sorry."

"What do you mean you're sorry? You kissed my head." She traced her marks on me. "I just whipped you, and you kissed my fucking head."

"You just *hugged* me."

She swallowed. "To stop all that shaking. I thought you were going to pass out, and I need you awake."

I labored a smile at her lie. She grimaced and stepped back, her eyes dipping to where she shouldn't be looking. "I can't believe you right now."

"If it bothers you this much, you should put some clothes on me."

"Or maybe I should chop it off."

She wouldn't. *Would she?* "You need me in one piece for the trade."

She grumbled, knowing I was right, and I wanted to laugh. I was too tired, tough. "Why the hell do you keep getting hard, you asshole?"

"'Cause all this shit you're pulling is driving me nuts. It hurts like fuck, and I hate you for it, but… I don't know." I shouldn't tell her how I really felt. I shouldn't let her take any advantage of me or make her think she had any power over me. All what she was doing could be an act to soften up to her and give her what she wanted.

"I can't stop thinking about kissing you." That was all I volunteered…to see if she was really trying to trick me.

The truth was, though, there was a lot more to what I wanted to do to her either way. Whether I liked it or not, I was attracted Cameron. Not that blonde chick I kissed in the backseat of her car, but the wild woman who tricked me and held me captive.

CHAPTER 16

CAMERON

I wanted to kiss him, too. To touch him. To feel the heat of his body on mine. To throw myself in his arms and…

"You're playing me," I whispered. *Of course. I show him one sign of kindness and he takes me for a fool.*

I didn't know what maddened me more. The way he underestimated me, thinking he could manipulate me with some sentimental lies, or my own stupidity, believing for a second he might have been genuine about what he said.

My own desire for it to be true.

He closed his eyes, exhausted. "I can say the same thing about you and that hug."

"I was whipping you for fuck's sake. Why would I hug you if…" *if it wasn't real?*

"And I swear to you I'm not lying."

My hands balled into fists. "You're full of shit."

"Maybe, but dicks don't lie, Cammie."

I blinked. Calling me *Cammie* with this masculine, lazy voice of his made my skin tingle. "Don't call me that."

"You don't like it when I pet you, sweetheart?"

"Fuck you."

He chuckled, opening his eyes. They settled lower than they should have. "Last time you had a tank top on, so maybe you were a little chilly. Now with the sweatshirt… You know nipples don't lie either?"

My eyes widened. Heat burned my cheeks. My arms moved quickly to cover the evident proof of my desire for him, but I stopped them midway.

I let my hands rest on my hips instead. No more hiding. If he was playing me, I'd better beat him at his own game.

"How about I make you an offer, Dusty?"

"An offer?" he chuckled.

"Since you're genuine about your attraction to me, I want to prove to you I'm not playing you either and all I want is the information that will let me get my sister back."

"How?"

I took a deep breath, summoning all my courage to do something I'd never done before. "How about a little show just for you, and all I want in return is that you tell me where they're keeping my sister?"

He winced. "Cameron, why can't you believe I—?"

I raised a hand at him to stop talking, impersonating Chelsea with all her firmness, confidence and assertion. "I think you'll change your mind and give me everything I need when I…" I went to the bag of toys and got out the first vibrating dildo I found. When I glanced at him, his tired eyes sparkled with life. I swung the toy playfully and plastered a smile on my face. "Would you like me to use this on me while you watched?"

"Fuck," he murmured.

"I think it'll be more than enough in exchange for that tiny little piece of information I need from you, right?"

He swallowed, his cock standing rigid.

I took the whip and gave him a little lash on the thigh. "Right?"

"Yes," he groaned.

"Good boy."

CHAPTER 17

DUSTY

I was too much of a dick to tell her to save her breath. Literally. What was still running of my blood rushed down to my cock, and I was reduced to nothing but that mother fucking anticipating erection.

The idea of watching Cameron play with herself was so fucking hot. Pleasure and torment all in one, knowing I couldn't touch her, and maybe a punishment afterwards when she realized I wasn't so much of a help to give her what she was demanding.

She started unbuttoning her jeans, hesitant at first but growing confident with every move. She had nothing to be insecure about. Didn't she know she was perfect, and right now, she had all the power?

She slid her jeans down, and I bit my lip at the sight of her thighs. I pictured the moment I'd spread them apart and dive nose deep between them, the moment I first smelled her, my first taste of Cammie.

When she got out of her jeans, I couldn't take my eyes off her beautiful body and the outline of her pussy, wishing I could tear the flimsy fabric of her black underwear off. She turned, gifting me the gorgeous view of her ass. "Fuck."

Her eyes met me over her shoulder. "You said something?"

"Yes, I said fuck. You're so fucking beautiful."

She tucked her hair behind her ear and went over to the chair. When she sat, she leveled her gaze with mine. "If you were no longer chained at my mercy, and I was standing in front of you unarmed, would you still say the same?"

"I would. You are beautiful. But I wouldn't just speak, sweetheart. I'd show you how beautiful you were with physical proof."

She chuckled. "How physical?"

"I won't be gentle, if that's what you're asking."

"Didn't you say you could be sweet and gentle for me?"

"Not anymore."

"You'll make me pay for what I've done to you so far?"

"Oh, fuck yeah. You'll be the one in chains, stripped and whipped and—"

"Fucked," she finished for me.

The things I'd do to her... "It's no news I wanna fuck you. It's what got me here in the first place. And it's no news I'm no good boy."

"Bad boys get punished."

I wanted her to punish me. Only her. It didn't mean I didn't want to punish her back. I so fucking wanted to hear her scream. "I can see that, but so are bad girls."

She parted her legs, holding the toy in one hand, the other pushing her underwear aside. "I thought you said I was a good girl."

I sucked in a hiss, my eyes zeroed in on her pussy. "I was wrong. You're a very bad girl...but when I'm outta here, I know how to make you my good girl."

She gave a mocking moan. Then she rubbed the tip of the dildo teasingly against her pussy. My tongue swiped across my rough lips, and I hissed again, imagining it was my cock teasing her instead.

Her lips parted with a little gasp as she let the toy slide inside her. Involuntarily, I tugged at the chains. The cold that reached my bones now shifted into heat washing over my body in waves.

Her gaze smoldered as she played with herself, pushing the vibrator in and out of her pussy without turning it on yet. Her gasps quietly but rapidly turning into moans—genuine, horny moans. I rattled my chains harder, wishing I was the one inside her.

Sweat formed on my forehead, and she took me in. Her gaze raked my body from head to toe, taking its time for Cammie's pleasure. The feeling was odd but so arousing. Being the object of a woman's pleasure with zero control on my side. A woman who was my enemy. She, literally, could do anything to me, and I couldn't stop her. It was dangerous, humiliating and sickly twisted but so fucking hot.

I had no explanation why it was turning me on. I should want nothing, think about nothing, but how to get out of here and ruin this bitch's life with the worst kinds of revenge and then kill the fuck out of her for what she'd done to me. But here I was, a marked toy for her pleasure, a sucker for her punishment, thirsty for more.

Her eyes grew even wider, glazed with hot arousal. She wasn't just putting an act to get me to answer her question. She fucking enjoyed it. "You like that, don't you?" I groaned.

"What?" Her rasp was heavy when she was in heat. It went straight to my swelling balls.

"Standing helplessly for your sick pleasure. A piece of fucking meat to eye fuck."

"If the roles were reversed, wouldn't you enjoy it?"

I rocked my hips, lulling my head for a second, and then whipping it back to her, my whole body simmering. "If the roles were reversed, I wouldn't just eye fuck you, baby."

"You tied women before for your pleasure, Dusty?"

"Yes," I sighed.

"You liked it?"

I nodded, taken by the glistening around the dildo. She was so fucking wet.

"Is that what you did to Annie?"

Jesus Christ. "What the fuck? No," I snapped.

"You never had a girl against her will?"

"Never," I answered firmly. I didn't know why I cared, but I wanted to make sure she believed me, at least, in that matter.

"Not so very Night Skull of you."

"Fuck! I told you I left. I was never—"

"You were never like your father or your brothers?"

"Yes. For fuck's sake, yes!"

"Where are they keeping my sister, Dusty?"

My eyes squeezed shut as I blew out a long breath. What the fuck was I supposed to tell her? That Roar had her sister as a gift for me and when I left he tossed her around? Or worse?

If Annie wasn't working the bars or the strip clubs like Cameron said, she would have met two destinies worse than each other. Annie would have been sold by now or fucking dead.

"Where is Annie? We had a deal," she said.

"You promised me a show. A show ain't one if you don't finish," I stalled. The truth would ruin everything.

She rolled her eyes. "You want me to come?"

"Yes."

"Tell me first."

"I'm not an idiot. Once you know, you'll be out of here. You gotta hold up your part of the deal first."

"Is that so?" She puckered her lips. "Okay."

"Okay," I whispered.

She switched on the vibrator, and her eyes drooped. It must have felt so good inside her, but I'd fucking feel better. *Sweetheart, when I'm done with you, you'd feel me for days.*

Her back arched, and she used the hand that held her panties aside on her tits. Then her hips rocked against the toy, and my balls screamed at me for a release. She stared at my angry cock, pre-cum dripping from the crown. I snarled like a caged animal, the chains yelling over the vibration of her toy. "Jesus fuck. Just unchain me for a few minutes, Cammie. Just one hand."

"So you can jerk off?"

"My balls hurt like fuck. I need to come, and I won't tell you where Annie is until I do."

Suddenly, she stopped the toy, put it aside and stood. "That's not what we agreed on."

"Don't give a shit. So unless you wanna give me a hand…"

She sauntered toward me. "You seem to have forgotten your place."

"You can't put a show like that and leave a man hanging."

Her gaze dropped to my cock and she smiled. Then she slapped my erection dragging a groaning curse out of me. She picked up the whip and used it on my balls.

"You vindictive bitch, I'm gonna kill you!"

"I thought you were gonna fuck me first."

"Holy fuck. You're so…" God, I'd never hated a girl as much as I hated her. Never wanted to fuck a girl as much as I wanted to fuck her. Never wanted to kill someone as much I wanted to kill her. Never wanted to protect anyone as much as I wanted to protect her.

"I'm so what, Dusty?"

"Confusing me."

She narrowed her eyes at me, studying my expression as if she was the one confused now. "You can end this confusion with one word. You tell me where Annie is, I arrange for the trade, and we never see each other again."

I could just lie and tell her anything and get it all over with. I could tell Roar never to touch her and let her go away from all our darkness and toxicity. But I was no saint, and never seeing her again was the last thing I wanted. I was never gonna let her go. Not before she was under me begging for mercy. Not before I was at her feet begging for redemption.

"No?" She sighed. "Fine. I have a better offer for you."

"What? You'll blow me or ride me?"

CHAPTER 18

CAMERON

My hand lifted to the smattering of dark hair across his chest and slid across the curves of his muscles, then down to the firm abs. My fingertips teased along the V that led to his pubic area.

His breaths hitched. "What are you doing?"

"What any person would do to the one they kidnapped." I glanced up at him, his eyes fully alert now.

His stomach rose and fell under my touch. "You can't be serious."

"Can't I?" I touched him along the edge of his inner thigh and continued backward to his ass.

Cold and solid as a rock, it clenched, reflexively. I had to break our gaze. Another moment and he would see how much I sucked at this game. How much power he had over me even whilst immobile and tied up.

The nervousness. The sound of his accelerating breaths. The firmness of his ass. The hardness jutting from his pubic hair. All went straight to my already drenching pussy, and set my nipples stiff to the point of pain.

My feelings at the moment perplexed me. Why on earth would I want the son of my sister's abductor? Why did knowing he couldn't help getting hard for me, even in these circumstances, set me on fire?

I squeezed his ass with both my hands. His lips parted, but no words came out. Only stammering.

My grip tightened around the cheeks. "What? You don't like it, *sweetheart*?"

He squirmed, trying to break free, inducing a stronger grip from me. "Fuck. If you wanna get laid, get me out of this shit, and I'll give it to you. Like a man."

"Till your gang figure out you're gone and come look for me, you're not a man. You're my captive. My fucktoy. I'll play with you however I want whenever I want."

He growled like a wounded animal, his body jerking right and left, shackles chiming.

I giggled. "How does it feel, Dusty? Standing all helpless, knowing you're about to get fucked? Raped by a woman half your size?"

"Don't do this…please."

"Please?" A surprised laugh escaped my chest. "That's new."

"What, do you want me to beg you? Do you like to be begged? Is that what it is?"

My nails dug in his flesh. "Do it, bitch. Beg me not to fuck this ass."

"Shit. Please, Cameron…I beg you. This is…"

The struggle in his voice to beg for the first time was music to my ears. "This is what, Dusty? Sick? Fucked up? Disgusting?"

"Yes!"

His cock begged to differ, sinews engorged along its girth. Thick wetness gushed between my legs.

"Tell me why I should listen to you?" I asked. "Did you listen to Annie when she begged you not to rape her? Did you stop?"

"I never laid a hand on her," he spat.

My hands fell off him, my eyes wide. Until his tongue had slipped, all I had was doubt and limitless unanswered questions. Now I knew for sure they took her. The Night Skulls did have

Annie. My chest heaved with emotions, a mixture of relief and horror. "Then who did?"

He pressed his lips and scowled in regret. "I don't know."

"Tell me, Dusty. What happened to her?"

"I swear I don't know."

I screamed as loud as I could, beating on him with every ounce of strength I had in me. He took it without making a peep. Blinded by rage, I spun and dove inside the bag. I couldn't take another second of this shit.

"Cammie, please."

"I said don't call me that." I took a ball gag and stuffed it inside his mouth. Then I used the electroshock on his thigh and his chest. Repeatedly.

He moaned, flouncing like a fish out of water. I undid the gag and repeated my question. The answer remained the same.

I secured the gag around the back of his head a little too tight this time. Drool trickled down his chin. His hardness wasn't deterred. "You like this, don't you? Okay. Let's see if you're going to like the next one."

A leather collar was visible from the bag, and I grabbed it without hesitation. I wrapped it around his big neck and buckled it.

The veins bulged under his tattoos, his back arching, as he struggled to breathe. I waited and counted thirty seconds in my head before I unbuckled the collar. Then I took off the gag and asked him one more time about Annie.

When his answer was nothing but a red face and a wild cough, I choked him again, increasing the duration ten seconds at a time until I reached one whole minute.

Still, he wouldn't break.

I knew what would break him. Not the electroshock or the whip or the collar. Not even the CBT devices. The strap-on. And it was right there, staring at me.

The only problem was I couldn't bring myself to do it. I'd hoped beyond hope the other tools would do the job so I wouldn't have to do this god awful shit. Violating him would leave a mark on his soul that would never go away. A scar for life. How could I do that to him? To anybody?

Annie's face flashed in my head. I pictured her asking me why the fuck I cared. Did he or any of his gang care about her? Did they think twice when they hurt her? When they violated her?

I was betraying my sister with my reluctance. My humanity. My care for that man. Yes, I cared about him, not just aroused by him, and it infuriated and terrified the hell out of me.

Exhaustion and trepidation overcame me. I had to stop to catch my breath. I took my phone out of my pocket and took a picture of him. Gagged, bound and choked.

Wild desire roiled in me as I looked at him like that. It was funny how things worked. I had to commit a crime, kidnap a man and torture him to know I had a kinky, sadist side and affinity for bad boys.

He said something, but it was hard to make it out clearly with the gag. It sounded like he was asking why I took his picture.

"Looks like I'm not going to get much out of you." I nodded, organizing my thoughts, weighing my options. "And something tells me it's going to take longer than I thought for your gang to come look for you. It's been two days, and they haven't showed up yet. Maybe I should expedite things on my own."

A flicker of dread darkened his eyes. He mumbled some incoherent words, shaking his head. I slid the phone back into my pocket and went to ungag him.

"Don't send them that photo. They're going to torture you to death. Please. If Roar sees what you've done, he'll make you beg him to end your life," he pleaded.

"Why the fuck do you care what they do to me? Don't *you* wanna do worse to me anyway?"

It was a moment or two before he spoke. "You don't know anything. I don't want you to get hurt, Cammie."

Something in his voice went through me. For the first time since I'd taken Dusty, I believed him. What a fucking idiot. "Stop playing me."

"I'm not. Don't believe anything I say, but believe this. I don't want you to get hurt."

I blinked, swallowing. "They're going to hurt me anyway when they find out it was me who took you."

"Not like that. You don't know what he's capable of."

"I do." Tears burned the corners of my eyes, so I twisted, heading for the exit. "That's why I have to get Annie out of there as fast as I can."

CHAPTER 19

DUSTY

"Cameron, wait." My voice trailed behind her, but she kept going.

The idea of Cameron in Roar's hands sent me spiraling, ripping my heart to shreds. The terrors she would see. I couldn't let that happen.

Not to her. She was mine even if she didn't know it yet, even if she'd never forgive me. I wouldn't let anything happen to her. I had to stop her. I had to protect her any way I could. Even if it meant telling her the truth.

"Please, listen to me. The night I saw Annie she was still a virgin," I confessed.

She paused for a few seconds, and then she wheeled back to me. "How do you know that?"

"Because…" I couldn't bring myself to say it. How could I explain without telling her I was the reason behind her misery and her sister's?

Tears spilled down her face. "I can't take this anymore. If you really care about me not getting hurt, you have to tell me everything right now."

"I only saw Annie once. The night I returned to Rosewood eight months ago."

"You did?" she sobbed.

"Yes."

Tears sprung to her eyes. "How did you know no one hurt her?"

I tried to swallow, but my mouth was too dry. "She was… Roar brought her to my room. He assured me no one else had touched her before."

"Your room?" Her sobs filled the silence. "What did you do to her?"

"Nothing. I swear. I didn't touch her. That night I left Rosewood and never went back."

She wiped her face with the back of her hand. "Why?"

A lump clogged my throat.

"Why?" she cried out. "It must have something to do with her. What the fuck happened?"

My eyes squeezed shut. "I was supposed to…" I tilted my head back, biting my lips. "She was taken as a gift for me."

I said it. I finally told her my secret, and it felt like I removed a boulder off my chest. Slowly, I opened my eyes, dreading her reaction.

She was bursting into tears, her arms folded around her like a protective circle. Her pain led straight to my soul.

"I'm sorry. I'm so sorry. I had no idea Roar would do that. I couldn't be a part of it. I couldn't be a part of any of his shit. I took off that night, leaving the Night Skulls behind me forever."

Her head whipped up. Her bloodshot eyes glazed with tears and rage. "And you left her there? You left her for them? If you really couldn't be a part of it, why didn't you get her out? Why didn't you take her with you? Why?"

Cameron's words and the image of Annie begging me to rescue her that night tore at me. "I'm sorry. Please let me help you get her back. I can and I will get her back for you."

"You'll say anything to make me set you free. You think I'm that stupid? You think I'll fall for it, you sick bastard? They took her for you, and you were gone. They would kill her." Hysteric rasps wheezed out of her. "She could be dead by now, you fuck. She could be dead." She scurried to the bag and yanked out a fucking strap-on. What the fuck?

"No. No. No! Cameron... Cameron! You can't do that."

She got into the leather harness and attached the fucking dildo that was inside her a few minutes ago to it. "I can, and I will."

I pulled the shackles around my wrists with all the strength I had left in my numb arms. My ankles pushed against the other set of chains. Fuck. These things were ironclad.

My breaths snagged as she approached me from behind. Although the collar was loose around my neck, I gasped for breath as if it was buckled, pressing down on my neck.

I felt her hands on my ass and a draught between the cheeks as she pulled them apart. Clenching my asshole as hard as I could, I begged her not to do this to me. She ignored me. Then Annie's image assaulted me.

Cameron was right. I didn't listen to her sister's pleas, why would Cameron listen to me? I left Annie to the most brutal men I'd ever known, to a destiny worse than death. Why should I be spared?

This was payback, and I should take it without a word. I deserved it.

The friction of the silicone between my ass cheeks sent a shiver down my body. The dildo tip reached my asshole, and I held my breath. She pushed. A tear escaped my eye involuntarily.

I was a man about to get fucked by a dildo worn by a woman, and I felt like shit. Imagine what that little girl had felt when a big man like Roar or any of the brothers shoved their filthy dicks inside her. More than once.

I didn't have the right to ask for forgiveness or beg to be saved. After allowing what happened to Annie, I didn't have the right to live. My ass stopped clenching. I gave up. Cameron should punish me however she wished.

She was pressing but hadn't entered yet. Her whimpers hurt me more than the persistent stretching the dildo was forcing upon my rim. The sobs grew louder with every push, wounding me. I hated myself and my family and my life. I hated everything, but Cameron.

Another tear fled my eye. Then cold air replaced the nasty, warm silicone in my ass. "I can't do this," she whimpered as her grip left my hips. "I can't."

I tilted my head as far as I could to look at her. She was crumbled on the floor, her head in her hands, weeping.

A scream burst inside my chest. Despite what I did and all the pain I'd caused her, this beautiful, caring, sweet woman couldn't bring herself to hurt me. Not in that vile way.

Roar wouldn't have hesitated to fuck her sister. Wouldn't have felt a shred of guilt. Would have bragged about raping a fifteen-year-old. Would have done it again and again without care or remorse.

Yet she couldn't do the same to his son.

"Cameron, come here."

She took off the strap-on and tossed it on the floor. "Leave me alone."

"No. Please. Just come here. I beg you."

Sniffling, she scrambled to her feet and faced me. "What do you want?"

"If I could, I would have you in my arms right now and never let you go. So please, come close. Let me feel you, Cammi—Cameron."

Her eyes glistened, and she couldn't stop crying. She threw herself on my chest, her arms tight around my waist, her tears burning my skin. I pressed my body to hers as much as I could. She met me with equal pressure, as if she needed this embrace more than I did.

I bent my head forward, straining my neck to kiss her forehead. As my lips touched her, she looked up at me. Then her stare dipped to my mouth.

My heart pounded against my ribs as the distance between us inched closer. Her sweet breaths teased my lips. Her hands reached behind my neck and bent me farther down, and then she stretched upward.

Our lips touched, hers too soft against my chapped ones. I kissed her hard. Devoured her. I didn't care if I was too rough. I needed that kiss. I needed *her*, and it was the only way I showed her how much I did.

When she pulled away, her lips were dark red and swollen, her breaths catching. She didn't say anything for a while, her eyes never leaving my lips. I held my breath. Was she going to let me kiss her again? Or slap my face?

She finally looked into my eyes. "I like it when you call me Cammie."

Battered, dehydrated and blown away by that kiss, I mustered the most sincere smile I could give her now. "And I like you, Cammie. A lot."

Her eyes were still shiny with tears, but she smiled back. She examined my arms. "You're getting purple. I'll go get the keys to the shackles so you can move those limbs before you lose them. Some food and water, too. You must be starving. And something to wear."

"Tired of watching my hard-ons?"

She bit her lip on a chuckle, already moving. "I won't be late."

"Cammie?"

She glanced at me over her shoulder. "Yes?"

"Has it really been two days since you got me here?"

"Yeah. It was Friday night when we…met. Today is Sunday." She checked her phone. "And it's almost eleven p.m. now."

"Just be careful. I'm sure Roar keeps tabs on me. My bike is still at the Belle View. Someone must have noticed by now."

She nodded.

"And don't send the photo. Just arrange for the trade. I won't tell them anything. We'll get your sister back, and I won't let anyone hurt either of you."

Her lips puckered. "If she's still alive."

She had to be. Rescuing Annie was my only chance to save my life and Cameron's. To make amends and win Cameron's heart.

CHAPTER 20

CAMERON

I locked the steel door that hid Dusty from the world and walked the dark tunnel, using my phone as a flashlight. Two things haunted me as I climbed the ladder well that led to the backyard of my Dad's house.

One: my sister could be dead by now.

Two: After everything that happened tonight with Dusty, especially after that kiss, my feelings for him could be my downfall.

Who kisses like that? With such power? With such vigor and passion?

Heat traveled from my core to my cheeks as the moment our lips touched washed over me. My mind had gone blank, and my knees had wobbled. I'd lost myself in that moment. Forgot who he was. Who I was. What we both had done.

I reached the last rusty rung and pushed open the hatch. Then I pocketed my phone and pressed my hands on the opening edge, shifting my weight up. My head peeked inside the back area of Dad's old Challenger, where there used to be a leather backseat. I had taken it out six months ago—since the police closed Annie's case—and made this hole in the bottom so I could go in and out without being noticed.

I cried when I made the alterations to the Challenger as much I'd cried the day Dad took his own life two years ago. I loved that car so much. It was the only thing he'd left us beside the house. Sometimes when I got into the driver's seat, I could still smell him.

After Annie, nothing mattered, though.

The Challenger was the perfect camouflage. No one would suspect that old, abandoned car in the backyard hid a big hole underneath that led to a secret tunnel and a covert bunker. And if someone saw me getting in and out of it frequently, they would just say I'd missed my dad.

I'd dug the passage and built the whole thing from scratch by myself. Courtesy of the three years I'd spent in engineering school, it wasn't such a hard task. Exhausting and time consuming, but not hard. My education, though unfinished, didn't go to waste after all.

I slid to the front seat and got out. Darkness covered the backyard and spilled inside the house. I turned on the lights and made a beeline to the kitchen. A bag of chips or a can of beans wouldn't sustain that stud after two days of starvation. He needed real homemade food. Meat to be exact.

A dreadful click murdered my thoughts. A sound I'd been anticipating for two days. Until a few minutes ago when Dusty's lips messed me up.

I stood still as the cold muzzle of the gun that had just clicked bore into the back of my head.

"Where's my son?" A rough, husky voice asked quietly. Roar's. His voice and face would be carved in my memory until the day I died.

An annoying static hummed in my brain. Everything was going according to plan. Until that kiss. Now, all my thoughts were muddled. My feelings, too. I'd been preparing for this moment for six months, for the time I'd be asked that question, the time I'd be taken, too numb, too angry to be afraid. But Dusty had ignited my soul, awakened emotions I didn't even know they existed.

Now, I was afraid.

If I let Roar take me now, Dusty would have no idea where I went. He'd think I'd lied to him. Played him. Besides, God only knew how long it would take Roar to break and give me Annie back. In his current condition, Dusty could wind up dead.

What the fuck had I gotten myself into? I'd never meant for Dusty or anyone to die? I just wanted to save my sister. If I didn't let Roar take me, any chance I had left to get my sister back would be lost. What was I supposed to do now?

Unless…

Please let me help you get her back. I can and I will get her back for you.

Dusty's words echoed in my head, but no. My trust issues screamed at me all at once. How could they not? Part of me was still skeptical about Dusty. He was Roar's son. A Night Skull. Everything he said, everything that happened between us could be a big fat lie.

How could I trust him or anyone including myself? I kissed the son of my enemy. I cared about him. My judgment was clouded. Obviously, I was no longer the Cameron I knew. I was not to be trusted.

Goddamn you, Dusty.

Goddamn your devilish lips and scorching body.

Goddamn your smile, your tenderness that outgrew your strength.

He had ruined me for life, and I was about to pay the price.

CHAPTER 21

CAMERON

"Where's my sister?" I finally found the courage to speak.

Roar grunted. "I figured leaving you alive would bite me in the ass later."

I stared at the refrigerator door in the dark, his shadow towering over me. "Why did you?"

I felt him grab my arm, almost dislocating it. Then he twisted me around and pushed me against the cold door. My head hit it with a bang, the gun pointed at my face now.

"'Cause you bitch set the cops sniffing on me. It'd have been too fucking suspicious." His obnoxious breath made me sick. He lifted his hand to my neck and squeezed. "Now, you gonna tell me where Dusty is or I'll make you beg for death before I blow your pretty brains up."

"You can't kill me," I rasped. "I'm the only one who knows where he is."

He chuckled. "He's gotta be here somewhere. Tearing this place upside down wouldn't be too hard."

"You think I'm that stupid so I'd keep him here?"

"Yeah, I do. A bitch that thinks she could kidnap my own son is one hell of a stupid bitch."

"Then go ahead. Knock yourself out." I put as much confidence as I could in my words.

The dim light spilling from the hall allowed me to see the wrinkles forming around the corners of his eyes as he glared at me. Never in my life had I seen such hatred in someone's eyes.

His long, blond locks fell over the sides of his face, covering it as he choked me harder. I could barely breathe. The guy was massive and strong as a bear. He could snap me in half without breaking a sweat.

I held my gaze, though, staring him down like my life had depended on it. It did, literally. If I didn't convince him he couldn't find Dusty without me, I'd have a bullet in my head.

"Fine. Let's see how long you'll last." His grip loosened.

Before I could breathe again, he threaded his fingers in my hair, pulling it. Then a heavy blow landed on the back of my head.

"I'll enjoy torturing your pretty ass." That was the last thing I heard before I fell to my knees, and everything went black.

CHAPTER 22

DUSTY

For the past two days, my body had begun to adjust to the conditions of this prison. Now everything was different. The cold was more unbearable after she left. Time moved like a fucking turtle. And the pain was just too much.

Looking at the color of my fingers and toes fueled my impatience. I closed my eyes. My mind replayed the moment I'd tasted her. A defense mechanism. Heat wasn't the only thing she'd given me with that kiss. She had given me hope.

Hope of freedom. Of the redemption I'd long sought after. Even the daring dream of happiness.

My eyes opened and stared at the sealed door, visualizing the second it opened with Cammie's beautiful face and killer body coming through.

Except that it didn't. She never came.

It must have been hours since she'd left, but my mind refused to believe she'd played me like that.

I like it when you call me Cammie.

And I like you, Cammie. A lot.

I rolled my eyes at how much of a fucking idiot I was. She wasn't coming back with keys or clothes or food. She wasn't coming back at all. She'd tricked me again, and I fell for it like a sucker dickhead.

But why? Why would she do this to me? To go on with her stupid plan that would only get her fucked? It didn't make any sense.

She must have been... NO! *Oh God, please no.* The second possibility set my blood simmering, yet my stomach felt like ice.

I was mad at her as much as I was scared for her. I didn't care if she'd played me. Again. I only cared about her.

Cammie would be in Rosewood, and that place was hell itself. Let alone if Roar found out what she did to me and took her by now.

Curses flew out of my mouth as I kicked at the fucking chains. I screamed my lungs out to push aside the images of the horrors my own father would do to the woman I… The woman I cared about more than I cared about my own life.

My sweet captor.

My Cammie.

If he does as much as touch her, I swear I'll kill him myself.

CHAPTER 23

CAMERON

The first thing I felt as I slowly regained my consciousness was cold air whipping my nipples. What the hell?

My eyes snapped open, and I realized I was stripped out of my clothes and tied to a pole with rope, arms above my head, the sound of male laughter synching behind my ears.

"She's up already."

Even though I was dizzy, and my head hurt like hell, I couldn't mistake Roar's voice. My body squirmed, struggling with the rope. My wrists and ankles burned. How long had I been out? It was still dark. A few hours tops? Shit. Was that how Dusty felt all this time? How he continued to feel?

My jaws hurt as I tried to scream. A gag had filled my mouth, leaving a nasty taste of rubber and dirt. The continuous supply of drool down my chin stung in the cold. I didn't need to feel my neck to know there was a collar there, too. Roar must have found Dusty's photo on my phone.

I'm screwed.

Please, let it be quick. For Dusty's sake. For Annie's.

Roar stood before me with his ugly smirk and the same hate for me in his eyes. Heels clicked behind me. Dusty's mother, I assumed.

With every step, I became more aware of the surroundings. I was out in the open. The pole was a tree trunk. There was a fire pit, already blazing, with empty beach chairs around it. What? Were they going to barbeque me and feast on me later?

The heels stopped. A woman in her forties, leather clad, stood next to Roar. She was definitely Dusty's mother. I saw where he got his looks. The dark hair and perfect cheekbones. The awesome lips. Mix the body of the grizzly blond with the face of that brunette and you get a heart-melting hotness named Dusty.

She stepped closer to me, smelling of cigarettes, weed and bourbon. "You've got a nice package here. The guys would be psyched to take turns on you. Hope you like gangbangs, sweetheart."

I wanted to swallow, and I wanted to spit on her face. I couldn't do either.

She came even closer, her hands suddenly on my nipples, twisting them ninety degrees. My eyes bulged as I shrieked in pain. "Fuck off, you crazy bitch."

She didn't seem to understand a word I said with that rubber ball in my mouth. Her fingers twisted around my stinging nipples again. My body jerked in place. She slapped me, and I swore again. So Dusty's mother was a psychopath, too? No wonder he left. There was no room for his warmth with these two.

Her hand squeezed the leather around my neck. "Shut up, bitch. The only thing you're allowed to say is where you're hiding my son."

Desperate for air, my nostrils flared, the pressing on my throat suffocating. I apologized to Dusty in my head.

When she let go of me, I wheezed. The freezing air lashed at my face and inside my chest. My gaze rolled up toward Roar. He was just standing there, giving me the same fucking look, his hands on his hips.

He wasn't looking at my naked body, which eased my trepidation. I wasn't afraid, though. Nervous, yes, but not afraid. Perhaps it was the adrenaline. Perhaps it was the power I had over this son of a bitch who took my sister. He was hurting over Dusty, and it felt so fucking good.

I wondered what their plan was. Good gangster, bad gangster. Was he supposed to be the good one or the bad one? I'd find out now.

"I take it you didn't find him on your own?" My lips moved around the gag.

He looked at the mother. "What's the bitch saying?"

Her fingers went behind my head, unbuckling the gag. I closed my eyes and jaws in relief. These things really hurt and gave terrible headaches.

"What the fuck you said? Where's Dusty?" she barked.

I ignored her and looked daringly at Roar. "I said I take it you couldn't find him on your own."

He looked like he was about to explode, but he remained still. His bitch blew up in my face. "I swear if you don't tell us where Dusty is right now—"

"You'll what?" I interrupted her. "If you lay another hand on me, your son will never see the light of another day. The only thing that will get him back to you is Annie. So why don't you be a doll and bring her out here already?" I glanced at

Roar again. "Clock is ticking. You all saw how I left him."

The giant monster couldn't take it anymore. He lunged at me. His big hand covered my throat and chin, the filthy fingers on my cheeks. "And I'll fucking kill you for that, but not just yet." His low, steady voice tied my stomach into a thousand knots. He laughed, as if he smelled my dread.

"Roar, what are you doing?" the mother asked.

The back of his other hand slid across my arm, and his gaze traveled down my nakedness. "I'm tired of this game. You're not scaring the bitch enough. Now it's my turn." His fingers glided down my side and between my thighs.

My body shook with violent tremors. It didn't matter how much I'd told myself whatever happened to me was a small price to pay for Annie's life, and she'd suffered worse. There was no amount of courage or practice or training that would prepare a woman for this kind of monstrosity. The moment I was in it, I'd forgotten everything. All I could feel was the agony of having an unwanted hand on my body. The horror that I was about to be raped.

He licked my cheek. He fucking licked me. I tilted my head away from him as far as I could, my eyes closed despite me. The wet feeling of his tongue on my skin flipped my stomach. Then he probed a couple of fingers inside me.

I wanted to scream. I wanted to cry. But I didn't. I clenched my hands into fists to control my shaking, and my vagina to prevent him from going any deeper.

"The bitch is tight." He shoved his fingers inside me.

Pain shot through my core. A scream burst out of me. I forced my eyes open and stared at him, my breasts heaving with every loud breath.

"This is not what we agreed on," his woman objected.

"Shut up." He held my gaze as he violated me with his fingers. He was enjoying it, savoring every moment of my humiliation. "I bet your ass would be even tighter," he told me.

I mustered the biggest phlegm ball I could and spat it on his face.

"Fuck!" He yanked his fingers out of me, scratching my folds, and wiped his chin. My spit splattered on the dirt when he shook it off his hand. The hand on my neck tightened. He was so strong I had to gasp for breath.

He shoved his fingers back inside me. My stomach turned, and I hurled its contents all over him.

"Son of a bitch! I'll fucking kill you right now!" he swore, and Dusty's mother swore with him. Repeatedly. He was no longer inside me or touching me anywhere. His fingers turned claw-like in midair as he stared down at the vomit covering his cut, T-shirt, jeans and combat boots.

As much as I was glad his filthy hands weren't in or on me anymore, sweat covered my forehead and trickled down my back, and I felt much colder than I already was. The vomiting wasn't planned, but it worked in my favor. However, I was afraid of his next move.

"Come, baby. Let me get you cleaned up first," Dusty's mom said, already linking arms with him.

He jerked her arm off him. "Not before I kill that bitch."

"We need her," she reminded him under her breath.

He growled. "Fine." His index finger jabbed in my face. "But when I return, you'd better have an answer for me, bitch, or you're dead."

He kept the menacing eye contact until he was satisfied, then he started. The threat didn't bother me, but with it came a revelation I never wanted to understand.

Not when Bianca couldn't look me in the eye when she said Cosimo couldn't help with bringing Annie back and stopped talking to me after. Not when I never found my sister at any of the Night Skulls' bars or clubs. Not now.

Not Ever.

Roar knew how much Dusty was suffering, and I was the only one who could free him. Why wouldn't he bring me my sister and end his son's misery? Why would he keep on threatening and torturing me instead?

It only meant one thing.

Cosimo didn't grant his wife's favor because he was protecting his business. He simply couldn't. Annie wasn't working the bars because...

"You don't have my sister," I murmured in disbelief.

The marching behind me stilled for a split-second. My heart skipped a beat. I waited for either of them to speak, to deny it, to lie, but the deafening silence was my answer.

"You killed Annie. You fucking killed my sister."

CHAPTER 24

DUSTY

The two days I'd spent here while Cameron was with me were a breeze compared to the time after she disappeared.

Nightmare after nightmare. A nagging question that wouldn't leave me alone. What if I never saw her again? What if he killed her?

Something inside me told me Annie wasn't alive, which meant Cameron wouldn't survive Roar's grip either. Every time I came to that realization, I lost my fucking mind. I tried to break the chains, each time fainter than the last, my strength betraying me. Then I cursed the day I was born. The day he was born.

Wasn't it enough to have the blood of a little girl on my hands? Now the blood of the woman I loved would be there, too.

Another realization that drove me insane.

I was in love with Cameron. How I worried sick about her safety and not mine, how my life meant nothing when hers was on the line, how much I was willing to sacrifice and who I was willing to kill to protect her, how I was ready to do anything to save her even if it meant my own death, proved I didn't just like Cameron, my captor, my enemy, but I was deeply and madly in love with her.

And I'd lost her. I couldn't save the girl I loved. The only girl I loved.

The flashlight had died out a while ago, but, desperately, I kept staring toward the door. "Please," I begged the emptiness. "Please, let her be safe."

The silence taunted me for what seemed to be an eternity. "FUCK!" I snapped at the chains, cursing my helplessness. I couldn't just give up. I wouldn't be able to live with myself if I did. There must be something I could do. A way out of here before it was too late.

I stared up at my wrists and the shackles secured around them. Those weren't cuffs I could break my thumbs to get out off, but it was worth the shot. I had to get out of here and a broken hand was a price I was willing to pay to save my girl.

One good thing about dehydration was that my wrist and fingers were shrinking a bit and the shackles weren't as tight as before. Screaming my lungs out, my famished, freezing body and the wounds blistering on my ankles screaming louder at me, I curled my thumb under the rest of my fingers and dislocated it. "Mother-fucking-fuck!"

Shaking and sweating, I squeezed as hard as I could to slip my hand out of the restraints, but goddamn those beefy hands that still wouldn't budge. Nauseated, I took a deep breath and decided I must break my pinky too. It was the only way, and I must do it fast before my thumb swelled and fuck everything up.

"Jesus fucking Christ!" I snapped my pinky and was on the verge of passing out. Biting my lip on the pain, I shook my head to stay awake. Then I growled, pulling my fucking hand down, the metal flaying my skin until my arm dropped as if it weighed a thousand pounds.

I couldn't believe this. My whole left side was searing with pain, but my arm was finally fucking free. One limb down. Three more to go.

I didn't mind. I was ready to take any kind of pain for Cameron. The one girl that brought me to my knees and owned my heart.

Suddenly, a noise like a distant key rattle penetrated the silence. It must have been my mind playing games on me.

More rattling. I blinked, startled. Then my heart skipped a beat when a familiar screech penetrated the never-ending silence.

"Cammie?" I called out.

The door swung open, the glare of incoming light sliced by one form. Not Cameron's. What the fuck? "Who the fuck are you?"

CHAPTER 25

CAMERON

Tears streamed down my face out of control. My jaws split apart as I intended to scream, but it seemed that I'd lost my voice for a few moments. Then a crescendo of sobs seeped out of my chest followed by a deep moan that sounded like wailing underwater.

Roar and his woman didn't utter a word, but their silence said everything. The confirmation my sister was gone.

Annie is gone.

All that time, she was dead. I'd kidnapped a man and hurt him, and now I was Roar's captive, who certainly would murder me. All for nothing.

Roar won. I'd lost everything. Even my own life.

"You fucking killed her!" I cried out hysterically, indefinitely, my insides contracting in pain, until I passed out.

In my unconsciousness, I saw Annie. She was riding her bicycle in a pink helmet and a white dress in Dad's house backyard. He was still alive, too. They were calling out my name, but I couldn't speak or touch either of them.

Then Sylvia appeared.

Anger shot through me. I didn't want to see that woman ever again. I swooped down on her, choking her, yelling how much I hated her. She felt like stone in my grasp. She just stared at me with no expression on her pale face. Then blood covered her head.

My hands let her go, and she rolled on her side, a giant, bloody hole visible in the back of her head.

I stumbled back as if I'd seen it for the first time. As if I didn't feel relieved the day she ended her miserable life.

Suddenly, it all came back to me, how I hated her even more that day, how I'd never shed a tear over her loss. Unlike Dad, she had seen no wars.

She hadn't had to kill people or watch her friends die or feel the fear of losing her life any fucking second.

She had no excuse.

The pathetic note she'd left after the police wouldn't look for Annie anymore said she couldn't stand the guilt of losing her. Guilt my ass. If she'd had any conscience, she wouldn't have neglected her little daughter and never noticed she was taken until the next fucking day. She wouldn't have left her other daughter alone in this life drowning in all that pain and grief. Sylvia had taken the coward's way out. Even at our darkest hour, she wouldn't stick around. I wished she'd lived to suffer the loss of her own daughter.

Like I should.

I'd left Annie, too. Her blood was on my hands like on Roar's and Sylvia's and Dusty's and Dad's. We all killed her, and we all had to pay for it one way or another.

I searched for Annie and Dad, but they'd disappeared. The backyard went dark, and I found myself in the bunker. Dusty was still there as I left him, shackled with a collar around his neck. He couldn't see or hear me.

Dusty? Dusty, please, talk to me. Why can't you see me? I touched him, but he didn't move.

"Dusty…"

Heat woke me up. I blinked at the early sun rays. The salty taste of my tears drifted in my mouth, mixing with vomit residue. Shooting pain hit me all at once. I tried to move my hands, but blood seemed to have left my entire arms. My feet weren't any luckier.

I arched my back, yanking my butt an inch away from the trunk. "Oh God." I bit my lip in pain. It felt like that tree dug a place inside my flesh and mashed with it. If I lived, I'd have bark marks on my backside forever.

A burning sensation spread through my vagina, and the dreadful memory punched me in the gut. That was when I noticed I wasn't alone.

"Had a nice sleep?" Dusty's mother, sitting in one of the beach chairs, was looking at me as if wondering how I could have slept when all this mess was going on.

How long had she been there? And why didn't she put out a cigarette in my chest to wake me up or something?

When I didn't answer, she rose and stood, facing me. "I'm Beth, by the way."

I hope you rot in hell, Beth. Scratchy and hoarse, my voice disobeyed me. My tongue felt like parchment. I was thirsty, and all the vomiting and screaming made it way worse.

"Don't be so cold, bitch. I've just told you my first name. Do you have any idea what the means?"

I'd studied MCs and their fucking codes for months so I did know what she was trying to do, but I played dumb.

"It means I'm risking my ass for you here to earn your fucking trust," she explained. "We never reveal our first names to strangers."

"And to what do I owe the fucking honor?" I slurred painfully.

She sighed. "I know you don't like me so much, but right now I'm your only friend." She leaned in to whisper in my ear. "The only one who can get you outta here."

Her smell nauseated me. Would my stomach flip again? I hoped it would.

"I'll help you, Cameron," she whispered.

"Help me?"

"Yes. I'll get you outta here in one piece. I can even help you leave the country and disappear." She pulled back and stared at me. "All you have to do is give me my boy back."

I sneered. "Let's say I'm too stupid to believe you, you really think I care about my life anymore?"

"You must. You don't know what he's going to do to you."

"Well, *Beth*, tell your monster to bring it, and…yeah…go fuck yourself."

She looked at me like a lioness about to pounce on its prey. But she didn't. "Fine. I have a better offer for you."

CHAPTER 26

CAMERON

"What fucking offer? The only thing I wanted was my sister, and you murdered her." Tears betrayed me.

"How about justice?" she asked.

Curious, I studied her expression. *Is she saying what I think she's saying?*

"You're not a killer, Cameron. You only want to avenge your sister. I get that," she said quietly.

"What are you saying?"

"I'm saying payback is a bitch. Killing Dusty will burn us, yes, but it won't get Annie back. It will only make a murderer out of you." She approached my ear again. "There's a better way to get your revenge. The right way."

I tilted my head, looking at her in disbelief. "You'll sell your man out to the police?"

She reached inside the back of her jeans and got out a gun. "Who said anything about the pigs?"

My heart thumped as I stared at the weapon in her hand. Would she do that? Kill her man? The father of her son? The leader of her gang? "How stupid do you think I am?" I raised my voice, and her eyes widened. "You expect me to believe that you'd ki—"

She pressed her palm on my mouth. "Quiet!" The panic in her eyes was real. "I'm trying to help you, you stupid fuck." Her voice was lower than the steady steps coming from behind.

"What's the bitch squeaking about now?" Roar grumbled.

"One word and you're dead," she mouthed and removed her hand, too certain I wouldn't rat her out.

Why wouldn't I? I could turn them on each other with one word and watch them fight. Who would win in the end? Would they both finish each other and spare the world their evil?

The idea alone was worth the risk. But there was some truth in what she said. The only reason

I wouldn't speak. I wasn't a murderer. Or so I liked to believe.

"I asked you a question." Roar's face appeared before me. My blood simmered with all the fury and hatred I had for this piece of shit.

Beth didn't speak. She just stared at me, unchanging, not even breathing.

I forced myself to look at Roar. "I was telling your ugly whore I wasn't falling for any of your pathetic, intimidating games. You can't kill me, so tell her to put the gun away."

"Oh yeah?" He grabbed me by my vagina. "Maybe we won't kill you just yet, but we'll do worse. You need another reminder of what happens when you don't do what I tell you to do?"

My skin broke into gooseflesh. I didn't close my eyes or look away, though. However, I wished I could have said I was less appalled by his forced touch. "Maybe you'll like my piss on your fucking hand this time?"

"The fuck?" He withdrew his hand and turned to Beth. "Where the hell does she get those disgusting ideas?"

"Who gives a shit?" She threw her hands in the air. "Just get her to talk!"

He glared at her. "Don't ever talk to me like that again."

"I'll talk to you however I want. You and the scrawny, little bitch you took are the reason behind this shit. If anything happens to him, I—"

He backhanded her so hard she flew backwards. "I said never talk to me like that again."

Her hand flew to her mouth. When she pulled it away, blood ran out of her nose and mouth. She was holding a tooth. Probably Roar's full fist broke her nose, too.

Beth shot up, the gun no longer in her grip. I scanned the ground for it and located it a few paces from where she fell. She struggled to stand steadily. "Just get me my son back. Now."

Roar clenched his teeth, grinding a curse. His fingers fished something from the inside pocket of his cut. A dagger with silver engravings of skulls and roses on the handle.

Startled, I held my breath, but my body wriggled. What was he going to do with that blade?

He held my tied hands in one fist and cut the rope with the dagger. Then he bent down and did the same with the bonds around my ankles. In my peripheral vision, Beth was stomping back toward the gun.

"Time to talk, bitch." He grabbed my hair and pushed me toward the pit. "But first you'll pay for barfing on me."

He hurled me over, and I fell to my knees against one of the chairs. I braced myself, holding on to the metal arms. "Do whatever the fuck you want to do with me, but I guarantee you will never see your son alive again."

His boot kicked my butt as I struggled to my feet, and I fell again, hitting the chair edge with my chin. Standing behind me, he gripped the back of neck and forced my face down. Then he stomped on my toes, squeezing a yelp out of me.

His weight on my toes was unbearable, and I thought I heard them crushing. My heart sank to my stomach when what sounded to be his belt unbuckling chimed in my ear.

"Let's see if you can say that again when you're left out here in the cold, thirsty, famished and bleeding your ass out," he said.

What? Was he going to fuck me in the ass?

My head jerked to the side, but he forced it back down. Everything was happening too fast, and I was in shock. I thought of something to say to literally save my ass. "Whatever it is, Dusty is going to die first."

He smacked me with the belt, the buckle heavy on my already sore skin. That would leave another mark. Another welt stung my thigh. Then my back and ass. At least, he didn't unzip his jeans.

"No, he won't, because you'll fucking tell me where he is right now." He whipped me so hard warm blood gushed down my back.

I moaned, my fists tight around the chair. I thought about fighting back, picking the chair and hit him with it. Maybe even try to escape Rosewood. But to what end?

I'd lost everything. No one to live for. Nothing to go home to. The future? What would I do with it without Annie? How could I live and start over knowing I failed to save my sister? My pathetic life wasn't worth saving.

Dusty's face flashed in my head. What about his life? Was it not worth saving, too?

I deliberated with myself for a few moments, the welts on my body too searing to feel the upcoming ones anymore.

"Wait." I raised my arm to stop Roar. It barely lifted above my head. "I'll tell you where he is under one condition."

The whipping stopped. He moved around me, yanking my hair to make me look at him. "You don't get to make demands. Where the fuck are you keeping him?"

The blood on my back trickled from one open wound to the other, burning it further. I curled my upper lip under my teeth in pain, Beth coming forward to where I lay.

Roar pulled my head harder. "Speak, bitch."

"I'll only tell you if you turn yourself in. Tell the police what you did to Annie."

He laughed. "Are you stupid or just plain nuts?"

"It's the only way to save your son."

"I have a better way." He dropped the belt and brought the dagger to my sight. He flipped it backwards, the engravings to my face. "Shoving this down your ass will get you singing like a canary, and if it doesn't, the blade comes in next."

My eyes bulged at Beth, Roar already behind me. Then the cold silver pushed between my butt cheeks.

I fought, jerking my body, my arms, my feet, but he was way too strong. He pinned me down and let the dagger tear at my rim. It was too big for me, and with my struggle, it wouldn't slide inside.

He put more force, and I cried. Unwillingly, I lifted my eyes to Beth, as if she was going to help me if I asked.

She was just staring at us, the gun low in her hand. The rough engravings inched their way inside my ass, injuring me.

I didn't have the will of the strength to fight anymore. Every part of me was distressed, and I was pretty sure I was about to die.

I'm sorry, Annie. I love you.

I snapped my eyes shut and waited for it all to end.

CHAPTER 27

DUSTY

"Don't move. My name is Alfarez, and I'm the only one other than Cameron that knows you're here." He pointed a gun at me. "If you do what I say, I can get you out. If you don't, you'll die right here."

That old fuck thought he could scare me? "Where the fuck is she? Why isn't she here? If you did anything to hurt her, I'll fucking kill you."

"Cameron is my friend. It's your family that's been hurting her. She didn't check in as we agreed, and when I came to see if she was okay I couldn't find her anywhere. That means one thing. The Night Skulls got to her before she could arrange for the trade."

"Fuck!" I pulled hard at the shackles on my right arm. "You gotta get me out of here. Now. I gotta save her."

He unlocked the safety switch on his gun, aiming it firmer at me. "You won't make another move until I make the call and set the meet or you're dead."

"No. You idiot, you gotta take me to Rosewood now. There's no time. If they have her and still haven't arranged for the trade yet, that means they have nothing to trade." They killed Annie like I suspected, and now Cameron must have lost the will to live, burdened by guilt so huge that she'd let them hurt her. "Please. I know how to get her out. I won't let anyone touch Cammie."

He narrowed his eyes at me and then swiped them over my free arm. "*Cammie?*"

It was nearly impossible to believe that the woman who kidnapped me now meant the world to me. How could I make him believe I was ready to die for her? "I care about her. I literally just broke my hand and was about to break the other and both ankles, without even knowing how to open or break that fucking door when I'd be crawling on my fucking ass, just for a chance to get out of here only so I can fucking save her. If that doesn't convince you that I'm on her side, I don't know what else can."

His skeptical stare gave me a flicker of hope, but every second we were wasting here was a matter of life or death for Cameron.

"Please, Alfarez. She's gonna die if you don't take me to Rosewood right fucking now."

CHAPTER 28

CAMERON

I let the pain swallow me as I welcomed death, Annie's face keeping me company. My only solace in this hell was that I'd see her and Dad soon.

In my heart, I apologized to Dusty, too. He'd be safe, though. Mr. Alfarez and I had agreed to check in twice a day. It must have been hours since I failed to do the last check in. He must have found Dusty by now and would take him out of the bunker soon enough. Taking Dusty to trade him with Annie was his idea after all. He was the only one I told where Dusty was in case things—like now—went south and I never made it out of here alive.

Killing Dusty was never on my agenda. In fact, my only condition to go on with that crazy plan was that Mr. Alfarez made sure Dusty would be safe either way. I couldn't have his blood on my hands even when he was my enemy, let alone when he was my…

Bang!

I flinched, blood dropping on my shoulder and back. Was it mine? Was I dead?

Suddenly, everything stopped. There was nothing in my butt anymore, and it hurt even more. I couldn't be dead if I still felt pain. Or heard sounds? Right?

A clink.

A big thud.

A faint kick on my bruised soles.

Another bang.

I finally opened my eyes and dared look behind me. The view took a second or two to register in my head. Roar was on the ground, his arms spread limp, a hole in his skull, another in his heart.

Maybe I died after all and was imagining all this.

I glanced to the side. Smoke was coming out of a gun. Not the one in Beth's hand. Her face wasn't the one filling my blurred view. It was Dusty's.

Yeah, I was definitely dead.

"Cammie. Cammie! Wake up! Cammie, I'm here." It was Dusty's voice in my ears as I was being shaken fervently. "You're safe. Wake up!"

I forced my eyes open, and Dusty was still there. A familiar warmth engulfed me. His, wrapping around me like a fuzzy blanket. "You're here? You're really here?"

"Yes, baby. I'm here, and you're safe now. You'll always be." He glanced at my naked body. He covered me with his T-shirt, sobbing. "Jesus fuck, what did he do to you? I'm so sorry. I wish I'd been here earlier. I'm so sorry."

"They killed her," I cried. "Annie is gone."

"I'm so sorry. It's all my fault. I'm so fucking sorry." Tears streamed from his eyes. "I'll do anything to make it up to you, sweetheart. He's gone now. He'll never hurt you again. I made sure of it."

"You killed him? It's you who shot him, not Beth?"

A commotion rose. Men and women in Night Skulls' cuts spilled from every corner of Rosewood. I was wondering where they had been all this time. Obviously, they had specific instructions not to come near me. I was too valuable, and only the king and queen were to handle me.

What was going to happen now? Was Dusty in danger for killing his own father to save me? Roar was the president, and all those angry Night Skulls were coming our way with malice in their eyes.

Beth looked at us, alarmed. Then she held Dusty's shoulder and took the gun from his hand. "No. It's me who killed him."

He shook his head rapidly. "Mama, no."

"Listen to me. It's the only way they'll let you live."

"She's my ol' lady, and I was protecting her. It's my right."

"You have no rights here. You lost your place at the table, you have no rank and they already hate you for leaving the MC. If they know you killed the president, you'll stand no chance at Church. But I will."

"How?"

The Night Skulls surrounded us like vultures. One of them, same age as Roar, crouched down next to Roar's body and checked his pulse. "He's dead."

"Who the fuck shot him?!" one of them shouted, and all eyes were shooting daggers at Dusty and me.

"I did," Beth said, her chest heaving. "He was about to kill my boy…and me."

Incredulous hums and questions rose around us. But Beth continued with her fabrications, unfazed. "Roar was forcing himself on Dusty's ol'lady…"

"When I arrived, I yelled him, telling him to stop," Dusty joined her, "but he didn't believe she was mine, so he continued hurting her."

"That's when Dusty and Roar fought, and then…" Her voice cracked so genuinely I almost believed her.

"He pointed a gun at me," Dusty finished for her. "Mama tried to take the gun from him, but he slapped her. I kicked the gun out of his hand, but he was stronger. He hit me and got it back."

"I couldn't think when I saw his hand on the trigger aimed at my only son," Beth sobbed. "I had to do something so I shot him."

"He fell to the ground, but the gun was still in his hand. He aimed at Mama," Dusty said.

"It was his life or mine. I had to shoot him." She broke with tears. "He left me no choice."

Before the gang started asking any more questions, Dusty called for the man who was checking Roar's body. His name was Rush and apparently he was the VP. "Cammie and me need help. Now."

"Go inside. Doc will help you," Rush said. "But this isn't over. Mama and you will have to face Church. Tonight."

"Understood." Dusty carried me, limping on his own wounds. He took me inside and put me in the shower. I curled up on the bathroom floor, shivering. Then sobs seeped out of me uncontrollably.

His arms cradled me. "Hey, it's okay. You're gonna be okay. I'm here. You're safe."

My eyes trailed on the blood covering the floor, and my sobs turned into loud gasps. He shielded me, pressing me into his chest. "Don't look. It's just you and me here. He's gone. I made sure of it. He's gone, and he'll never hurt you again. No one will ever hurt you again."

How could he be so sure? In this place no one was safe, especially not after what happened. What was going to happen to Beth? Would they find out the lies and kill her, too? Would Dusty and I be next in line?

CHAPTER 29

CAMERON

When I finally woke up and Doc finished patching me up and filling me with antibiotics, Dusty arrived to the room he'd put me in. Doc gave us some privacy and said he'd return with food.

"How are you now?" Dusty asked.

"Better," I said just to reassure him, but there was no medication that could heal the agony I was in. I clutched at the T-shirt one girl gave me to change the subject. "They were kind and gave me this to put on, and Doc is very skilled. He did a great job with the wounds." I stared at the cast on his left wrist. "He did your cast, too?"

"Yeah."

"I can't believe you broke your hand to get out of the shackles."

He wrapped his arm around my shoulder and stretched on the bed beside me where I lay. "To get to you. I was ready to break both my arms and legs just to get to you, Cammie." He blew out a troubled sigh. "I'm so sorry I was late. I wished I'd arrived earlier….before he…"

"You were trapped. I kidnapped you, and you still broke your own hand to protect me. You went through all this trouble because of me and still you made it in time…and saved me." Tears sprang from my eyes. "You saved me, Dusty. You killed your own father for me. Why?"

His tender eyes cradled me. "Because if anyone here deserves to be saved, it's you, baby."

"No. I hurt you, and now you and your mother are in trouble because of me."

He shifted, his arm dropping off me. Then he put on a faint smile that was far from genuine. "We're not in trouble. Not anymore."

"How?" I glanced at his outfit. He was in jeans and t-shirt, no cut. "Why aren't you wearing your cut? What happened at the meeting…if I'm allowed to ask?"

It was a moment before he spoke. "Well, they bought the story. But most of the brothers were really angry because some members at the table took Mama's side."

"And?"

"And…that caused a problem. The vote was in her favor, no retaliation, but the members who didn't vote for her didn't look so pleased."

"What does that mean, Dusty?"

"It means there's a division. With that comes mayhem. Someone could split or take matters into their own hands."

I frowned. "I'm sorry. Does that mean your mother is still in danger?"

"Don't worry. I won't let anything happen to her."

"Of course. So that means you have to stay here in Rosewood, back with the Night Skulls for real, right?" I didn't know why my heart squeezed. It was expected he'd stay with his family after what happened, and what Dusty did with his life was none of my business.

He nodded, his Adam's apple bobbing. "It's not just that."

"What else?"

He rose to his feet, a scowl on his face. "You're looking at the new president of the Night Skulls."

My eyes widened, yet my chest contracted. "What? H-how? They were angry at you, too, and, no offense, but you're too young. Shouldn't your VP be the president?"

"Yes, but…Rush didn't want to be the president. He nominated me and gave me the first vote."

"That's so weird. Why?"

"Because the Lanzas said so."

I blinked in confusion. "I don't understand. How can they have a say in who runs your club?"

"When I came back from Europe the last time, they came to me. They knew about my issue with Roar and didn't like that I was visiting other clubs. They wanted to make sure I wasn't gonna join a club they don't work with or start my own."

"So they told Rush to make you the president to ensure you're not going anywhere and protect their ongoing operations."

"And if I say no…"

"Your mother will be in danger. If they can sway the VP to do their bidding, they can sway the others to create mayhem."

"Exactly."

I dangled my feet away from the mattress, preparing myself to leave. "I'm so sorry about all the trouble I caused you and your mother. It's a lot to process. You probably shouldn't have told me any of that, but thank you for sharing and your trust."

"You're my ol'lady."

I glanced at him over my shoulder. "I appreciate you lying to your brothers so they can spare my life, but you don't have to do this when we're alone." I pushed myself up. "It's time for me to leave anyway."

"Leave?" He dashed toward me. "Cammie, no. I want you to stay. I want you to be with me, here, as my ol'lady."

I tucked my hair behind my ear and walked slowly to the door. "You know I can't do that."

He stopped me. "I know how hard it is for you to be here, but Roar is gone, and when it's me running things, you'll always be safe."

"I can't, Dusty. I can't be a Night Skull. Not even for you."

With a grimace, he shook his head. "I'm not leaving you."

"Yes, you are. Your mother needs you, and you have a club to run."

"Screw everything. Cammie—"

"It's over, Dusty. What we had was…something we'll regret for the rest of our lives. Now, we put it behind us and try to live with it. Both of us can finally go home…and heal."

"What about your wounds? Who's gonna heal them?"

"I can take care of myself."

"Why don't you let me take care of you? Heal together?"

I put my hand on his cheek, fighting back the tears. "Our worlds were never meant to cross paths. And I'm sorry for all the pain I'd caused you. I hope one day you can forgive me."

"I forgave you a long time ago."

"I just made you kill your father, Dusty. No matter how much you hated him, you won't truly forgive me for it."

"Is it strange that I don't feel as much sorrow for what happened to my parents as I felt for you and your sister? Is it weird that in the past three days I felt that I belonged to you more than I've ever felt with my own family?"

"Dusty…"

His lips swept over mine, melting me in their scorching heat. His hand tangled in my hair and pressed me harder to his body.

Swiftly, I drew back before I crumbled into his embrace and fell beyond redemption. "We can't… We were born enemies. We're supposed to hate each other."

"I don't hate you, Cammie. I don't think I ever did."

"I don't hate you either. I don't think I ever did."

"But can you forgive me? Can you forget who I am and what I did? Can you look past the tattoos on my chest and into my heart? Or will I always be the son of your sister's murderer? The coward that saved himself and left her in hell?"

"It's not your fault, Dusty. It's Roar's. It's the Night Skulls." I moaned. "I can forgive you, but I can't forgive them."

"Cammie, please don't go. I need you."

"Like I said, our worlds were never meant to cross paths. Goodbye, Dusty."

CHAPTER 30

DUSTY

I walked into the backyard I'd been locked underneath. Bad and good memories collapsed.

Until I saw her.

A smile forced its way on my lips like nothing ever happened. Like I'd never suffered in that bunker under this very house and neither had she.

She was hunched over the old Challenger, in a blue shirt and jeans, her hair a little longer than I remembered. It swirled behind her shoulders when she twisted and saw me.

This was the first time I'd seen her clearly in daylight when she wasn't covered in blood and my vision wasn't blurry with pain and rage. My heart rocketed, and I seemed to have forgotten everything I'd prepared to say. A fucking hard-on ached in my jeans. Sometimes, I hated this power she had over me.

I slowed down, hands in pockets, keeping enough distance between us. I wouldn't be able to resist crushing her into my arms and kissing her lips if I went any closer. "Hey."

She wiped her hands with a greasy rag, her eyes alert and darting behind me. "Hey."

God I missed that rasp.

I nodded at the car, wondering for the millionth time what kind of a diabolical mind she had to come up with the idea of using the Challenger to hide the bunker. "Fixing up this old thing?"

"Um-hum."

"What? Done kidnapping bad boys?"

She sighed, her lips twitching.

"How did you get me down there? You threw me down the hole and dragged me into that room?"

She cocked a brow at me. "If you're trying to record this, it's a pretty lame attempt."

"Record it? Why now, you think I'll rat you out to the pigs? That's offensive. If I wanna retaliate, baby, it won't be by sending you to the pigs." *It'll be tying her to my bed where I fill every hole she has for months, years…forever.*

"Well, in that case, as you know I had a person. They helped with that one detail. I didn't wanna risk a concussion."

Sweet from start to end. I smiled at her, at her beauty and kindness I missed so much. "How're you doing, Cammie?"

She shrugged, her expression a question mark, her gaze restless. "Okay, I guess."

I stepped forward, and she backed away. *Oh c'mon.* She was scared of me now? "I'm here alone, Cammie."

"Is that so?"

A lump clogged my throat, but I couldn't stay silent. "You really think I'd come here to hurt you?"

"I don't know what to think anymore."

"Well, I'd never do that, and you know it."

She bit her lip, nodding once. "You look good, by the way."

I swung my cast free arm. "All healed." I took her in and gestured at her body. "You look amazing."

"Thanks." She ran a hand through her hair. "Why are you here, Dusty?"

I smiled again, and she looked away, running from my gaze. "I heard you were going back to school."

She moved around to the passenger side. "Heard?"

"Um…" I ran a thumb over my brow, following her. "I mean…when you decided to cut ties, you left me no choice but to keep tabs on you for the past couple of months."

She swallowed, leaning against the car door. "Why would you do that? I'm not a threat anymore."

"C'mon, Cammie." I tucked her hair behind her ear. "You know what I'm talking about."

A soft tremble ran through her. She crossed her arms over her chest.

"Are you really scared of me?" I asked in disbelief.

She laughed under her breath. Then she finally held my gaze. "You know I'm not." Her arms moved nervously, and then she crossed them again. Not fast enough to hide those hardening nipples from me.

Oh.

My cock throbbed. Standing this close, knowing she wanted me too, shattered my resistance. I leaned in, devouring her lips with my stare before my kiss.

The fire inside her, the one I'd been dying to taste again for the past couple of months, set me in flames, even though she broke the kiss almost immediately.

"Dusty," she whispered. "*Why are you here?*"

I placed my hands on the car top, caging her, afraid she might run away. "I'm here to tell you don't go."

She blinked and took a deep breath. I struggled so hard not to look at her tits. "We talked about this."

"Don't go, Cammie."

"I have to. I lost my scholarship, and I've taken a fat student loan to go back to school. I must go and finish so I can get a job to pay for that loan."

"That's not a problem. I'll cover that."

She grunted, not pleased, her gaze at the new patch on my cut full of disdain. "And you'll cover it with what? Blood money? From the people who killed my sister?"

"Cammie, just give me a chance." I took her hand in mine and planted a kiss inside her palm. "I know I can't bring Annie back, but I can make things right for you again."

She pushed my arm and got out of the circle I made around her, but I didn't let go of her hand. "Let me go."

"No."

"What? *You* will kidnap me now?"

"If I have to."

She tried to pull her hand, inducing a firmer grip on my side. She bit her lips on a smile. "Just leave me alone. Go run your gang. You belong there."

She couldn't have been more wrong. "Tell me that kiss in the bunker wasn't real."

A deep sigh burst out of her mouth. "You know I can't say that."

I closed the distance between us and twined my fingers with hers, holding both her hands now. "Do you regret it, too, like you said you regretted everything between us?"

"I regret a lot of things," her breath hitched, "but not that kiss."

"That kiss changed me and my life forever. Made me know where I really belonged. *Who* I belonged to."

She glanced down. I lifted her chin with the back of my hand without breaking our hold. "Please don't go, Cammie. Just come with me. I'll do everything in my power to make you happy."

Her eyes reddened with tears. "I have to go. I have no one here anymore…and I certainly can't be a Night Skull."

"Things have changed since I took the lead, I promise."

"It doesn't matter."

I knew she was too damn stubborn. "Then I'll leave everything to Mama and come with you."

She stared at me, her eyebrows inched high. I squeezed her hands gently. "What? Surprised?"

"Dusty…"

Every time she said my name with that rasp, my cock jumped with a big twitch. "You don't have to decide right away, but I'm not leaving here till you know you're mine."

"What the hell? No, I'm not."

I pulled her into me. "Then I'm not leaving here until you know I'm yours."

Her breath caught, driving me nuts. "You're crazy."

"Crazy about you. My beautiful captor."

"Stop messing with my head. It's enough what you do to my body."

I couldn't help the grin on my face. "You kidnapped me, and all I've been thinking about since that day is how to stay with you and never leave. It's you who messed me up, Cammie. All of me." I cupped her face with my hands and pulled her more closely so she could feel what she was doing to my body, too. My erection was hard and heavy, and a little gasp came out of her chest as she felt it.

She looked at my lips. I liked the way her eyes stayed there. The way her tongue darted out and licked her own lip.

I couldn't wait anymore. I bent my head and kissed her. This time she didn't draw back or hold back. She matched my desire with sensational passion.

She surrendered.

Her hands hungry to touch me as much I was dying to touch her, she led me inside the house and into her bedroom.

Quickly, the body that occupied my wildest fantasies for months lay naked under me.

"You're so beautiful," I said, my heart racing as I settled on top of her.

She swallowed. "I have to warn you I'm not very good at this."

"What?" I shook my head with a smile. "I find that very hard to believe. Who told you this shit anyway? I'd go kick his ass."

She laughed, and her hands roved my body. "I missed seeing this."

"I missed you, too. So much."

I traced her skin with soft kisses. Felt her heartbeat in my palm. Tasted her.

She was too soft to be left unprotected. Too wild to be tamed.

"I love you, Cammie," I whispered into her mouth.

Her big eyes grew bigger. "What did you just say?"

"You heard me, sweetheart." As much as I wanted to hear it back from her, I didn't want to rush her or get her to something she didn't mean. I wanted her to love me for real.

Like I did.

At the same time, I was scared to hear her say she didn't feel me that way, so I changed the subject. "You still have that bag?"

CHAPTER 31

CAMERON

Dazed was a little word compared to what I felt since Dusty showed up today. And now that I was naked with him, listening to his rugged voice saying he loved me…

"Cammie? You know which bag I'm talking about, right?"

I knew what he referred to, but what the hell? He'd just told me he loved me. Or did I imagine it?

"What did you just say, Dusty?" I repeated.

He gave me his heart-melting smile. "I was asking if you still have your kinky toys, you crazy psychopath."

"Don't be a dick."

His calloused fingers caressed my cheek. "Does it surprise you? That I'm in love with you?"

My heart thudded. I didn't know what to say. What to think. He looked like he was waiting for my words, but I had lost them all. So I wrapped my arms around him and put all my emotions, the longing, the need, the confusion, everything in one kiss.

He swallowed, his face flushed, his cock glistening.

"The bag is under the bed," I said at last.

Swiftly, he rolled off of me and reached for the bag. The swoosh of it as he dragged it out and the squeak of the zipper sent a fresh gush of desire between my legs.

"I wasn't a fan of the electrics," he went through the toys, "or the strap-on." He glanced up at me with fake reproach, and I was screaming OMG in my head. How could he talk so casually about them? The tools I once tortured him with?

"But the tying up and the whip, even the collar," he continued, picking up a whip and a collar already, "I wanna try that again."

"You sure about this?"

He winked. "Absolutely."

"Won't that bring bad memories?"

He laughed. "The cock wants what it wants."

"Dusty, I'm serious." I was starting to worry about him. I wasn't a psychiatrist, but it didn't need one to see that something was wrong here.

"I'm serious, too. You saw what it did to me before."

My stare dipped to his erection. His massive hard-on that had haunted my masturbations for the past two month. "It doesn't look like you need any extra help with that."

"Maybe, but I really liked it, so why not?"

I sat upright. "Liked it? That's how you describe your experience being kidnapped? You *liked* it?"

He set the toys on the floor and held my hand, printing a kiss there. "I never thought I would, but honestly, there is something extremely hot about being under a woman's mercy. And when that woman is you… I mean, I've been dying to try all those kinks you introduced me to since you left, but I couldn't bring myself to do it with someone else. Actually, I couldn't bring myself to touch anyone else."

Holy smokes! A tingling spread through my body and into my sex. He, this charming, puff, all tatted, bad boy with the huge dick, who was now the fucking president of the Night Skulls, hadn't touched anyone else? Because of me?

He winked again. "I know you liked it, too."

"I did." I spoke without thinking. I could feel there was something seriously wrong with Dusty asking to replicate his trauma, but the responsible part of me was too clouded by the painful throbbing in my core to argue. There really was something extremely hot about having a man under my mercy.

Great. I was fucked up, too.

I shook my head in an attempt to snap out of it. "Dusty…I'm so flattered, but…this is classic Stockholm syndrome."

"I think you'll need more than three days to get that."

"Maybe, but…you're not even submissive."

"But I will submit to you. Only you."

He found some leather cuffs and showed them to me. "So what do you say… Mistress?"

I laughed under my breath, in a daze, as he handed them to me with mischief in his eyes. Then he crossed his hands together before me.

The marks on his wrists from the shackles were still there. "Dusty, I don't know about this."

"I need this. With you. I need *you*, Cammie."

The passion in his voice numbed my concerns. I needed him, too. My desire for him and his body, for what he was offering, was mutual.

I let him back on the bed, cuffed both his wrists and ankles, and placed a collar on his neck. When I turned to get the whip, he swore. I spun, unsurprised. I knew he would react badly when he saw the scars on my back.

His eyes glittered. "I wanna kill him again for what he did to you."

"Hey." I stroked his beautiful hair. "It's okay. It's over."

His jaws clenched. "I wish there was a way I could take it back."

Pushing the awful recollection of Roar and every fucking thing he did to us off my mind, I kissed Dusty's fleshy lips. "You saved me, Dusty. That's all you need to think about."

My lips found his again before I got on top of him, the whip in my hand. I started slowly, gently, gauging his reaction with every welt, every choke. He did like it. So much.

Cocks didn't lie.

And when he was inside me, filling me, stretching me, showing me what those fucking piercings could do—holy fuck—we were moaning together. Crying out each other's names with intensity I'd never experienced before.

It was amazing. Beautiful. Deep. Deeper than any other kind of pleasure. The trust, the submission, the vulnerability.

Not that I didn't equally enjoy it when I untied him and waited for him to recover so I'd feel him inside me one more time. Just the two of us, a man and a woman, with no tricks.

"You feel so fucking good, baby," he groaned as he stretched me, determined to give me every inch.

"You're too big," I breathed.

"But you're taking it so damn good." He glanced down at where we were connected. "Look at you. Look at the fucking tight little pussy taking all of me."

I hissed. "Fuck."

"Yeah, baby, that's it." He bit my earlobe as he groaned. "That's fucking it. Take it all like a good girl."

"I thought I was your mistress, and you were my good boy."

"You are, and I am, but right now, you're my good girl that's taking all my cock so fucking good." His big hand cupped my breast and squeezed as he slammed into me. The rings in his cock teased my clit in ways I couldn't imagine.

"Come for me, baby." His sexy groans, the hardware in his gorgeous cock and his experienced thrusts drove me to the edge. I dug my nails into his ass, and he gave me all of him until I was screaming with the orgasm he raptured inside me.

He came right after, and then we collapsed into each other's arms. I didn't think he was the cuddling type, but he held me with a sated smile on his face for what seemed to be hours.

"A penny for your thoughts," he said.

"I was wondering how a guy like you could be so gentle and caring."

"A guy like me? You mean a Night Skull whose father was—"

I shushed him. "I mean a guy who's used to taking and not giving because he's obviously desired and now even more powerful. I don't imagine you had to cuddle before."

"You're right. I don't *have to* cuddle. But with you, I want to."

"I can be sweet and gentle for you, baby," I imitated his voice.

He laughed and kissed me. "You're trouble. From the first moment I laid eyes on you."

I smacked his ass.

"Oh yeah? Okay." He rolled on top of me and slid down, holding me by the hips. Then he parted my legs, darting his tongue out.

"Oh my God, no. I already came three times."

He didn't heed my protest, and the wetness of his tongue took over me. I squirmed at first, asking him to stop, but then I had to surrender to the pleasure he drowned me in. Why was I complaining? His mouth and fingers squeezed another orgasm out of me, letting me know, while I was the one that tied him to my bed and held a whip, *he* dominated and owned my body.

Dusty was everything I ever needed and more.

"Maybe next time we do it in the bunker with the shackles and all?" He smiled.

"Too cocky. Who said there would be a next time?"

His expression darkened. "Don't ever joke about this."

I curled in his arms, surrounded by his warmth and incredible muscles, marveling at him. Whether there was going to be a second time or not. Whether we could be in a relationship after everything we had been through. Whether I'd go with him or he'd come with me. This wasn't the time for making such decisions.

This was the time for putting all worries aside and be happy. The time for hope.

CHAPTER 32

CAMERON

It was impossible to concentrate on the relationship between modulus of elasticity and strength Professor Lathery so passionately was explaining, though. I'd only slept for two hours last night. I couldn't help but zone out.

Getting back to college wasn't very difficult. In fact, it was the easiest part. CIT didn't take me back, but, among a few other places, Cal Poly accepted me. It was the perfect choice. Far enough—four hours—from home but not too far for Dusty to visit.

Even though he wasn't fully on board with my choice, I couldn't stay in San Francisco, not even for him despite how much I wanted to. Last year, I lost everything. My college scholarship, a huge chunk of my soul, the last member of my family, and almost my life to this city of pain. For a chance at starting a new life, with the man who said he loved me, the only man I ever wanted to be with, I had to leave all the dysfunction of my past behind, turn my back on the places, the people, the pain and run toward my future.

I was a semester and half away from getting my bachelor's degree, and I couldn't be happier—drowning in student loans and enormous amounts of worksheets but happy.

Except for the time when I was alone without Dusty. Damn those fucking nightmares. Every time I closed my eyes, the dreadful events of the last year haunt me like a fucking plague. Every night I woke up in the middle of the night covered in sweat, breathing as if an elephant sat on my chest. Then I try to remind myself that it was over. I was no longer in Rosewood. I survived. That must have amounted to something, or so I kept telling myself as I searched for a way to move forward.

To live.

"Annie…"

Someone whispered next to me, and a pang set in my chest.

All right, I wasn't happy at moments like these either. When I accidently heard someone call a girl who had my sister's name, or when Ashley, my roommate, asked me to braid her long, black hair, like I used to do with my sister, or when I saw an old blond man on a motorcycle…

Sometimes, I didn't even need a trigger. The ugly memories would sneak up on me unexpectedly. In the classroom. In the shower. At lunch with my college friends or the occasional party Ashley dragged me to a couple of months ago.

Lingering, like a disease.

I wished I'd been able to lay down the unfortunate baggage I was forced to carry into my future. I tried everything to forget. Bury myself in my studies. Drink. Smoke. Go on long rides on the new Harley Dusty bought me when I moved here.

But the memories stayed. Always there. Indelible. Unforgivable.

Eventually, I learned I couldn't forget, no matter how much I'd try. The best way to cope with the dreadful past was accepting it and counting my blessings.

I was able to get out alive.

I went back to engineering school.

I was in love—even when I hadn't said it to him yet—with a very tall, very handsome, packing, all-muscle hotness.

Who is also a motorcycle gang president and the son of your sister's murderer.

"Shut up," I said through my teeth.

Ashley took her feet off the bench in front of her and scowled at me. "I didn't say anything."

I nodded then shook my head, blinking. "Yeah… sorry."

"You're so edgy these days. What's going on?"

My gaze shifted to the professor and then landed on my textbook. "Just not getting enough sleep."

She sneered. "'Cause our Halloween slash Bloody Valentine, aka our only chance at Valentine's Day because we have mid-fucking-terms, is around the corner and you're missing Dusty's big—"

"The fuck, Ash?" I loved her but hated when she gushed over my boyfriend and his… package, especially after that morning when she *accidentally* walked in on him in the shower and saw him naked. All of him.

"Easy. It's not like he has eyes for anyone else but you, you lucky bitch. But we're friends. It won't hurt if you share him a little. He's got enough for both of us."

I laughed under my breath. "I'll kill you."

She stuck her tongue out at me then buried her face in her textbook, hiding her laughter.

I did miss Dusty, though. Needed him.

The last thing I wanted was to be dependent on anyone, let alone a fucking Night Skull, but I didn't know what I would do without Dusty at this point.

Despite our past, and my fears The Night Skulls would ruin him, turn him without noticing into another Roar, I had to submit to the fact that he was my rock. Without him, I was vulnerable and empty.

Even though our worlds would never fit together, and the chances for our relationship to work out were less than slim, he was all I had. Against all odds, I loved him with all my heart.

Professor Lathery dismissed the class, and I shoved my stuff into my backpack and headed out with Ashley. She linked arms with me as we strolled into the hallway. "He's gonna show up."

"Who?"

"The pope." She rolled her eyes. "Dusty. He's gonna come over for Valentine's."

"Nah. He called me last night saying he had a lot of work this week. He didn't even mention he remembered the party." I pursed my lips, frustrated, climbing down the stairs. "I don't think a guy like him celebrates the real

Valentine's Day or even knows it exists, let alone a sad, fake, geeky one on fucking Halloween."

A mischievous smile crossed her face as we got outside the building. "Wanna bet?"

She was wiggling her eyebrows, her short, petite body rocking with excitement. Before I questioned the reason, a bike engine revved on campus and through my heart. My head whipped toward the sound, and I saw Dusty on his Harley. I ran over to him, a huge grin hurting my face.

He gave me his mesmerizing smile, getting off the bike. Then, before I even reached him, he swept me off my feet and into his arms. His lips couldn't wait to devour mine, burn them with all the passion and the longing he had for me.

I inhaled the musky, leathery scent of him. The smell that took up permanent residence deep inside the corners of my mind and associated itself with arousal. One whiff, and my nipples turned into little pebbles. And with that kiss, I needed to change my panties.

When he finally put me down, I punched him lightly on his arm. "You said you were busy."

He took off his shades with one hand, the other remained on my waist, his bright eyes so fucking beautiful. "I wanted to surprise you." His eyes shifted over my shoulder as he smirked. "Hey, Ash."

"Dusty," she cooed.

I twisted, staring at her. "What the hell are you still doing here?"

She did that wiggly dance again, her long braid bouncing behind her back. "Wanted to say hi to Dusty."

"And you did. Would you go please?"

"Yeah, yeah. Just give me the keys to your bike. I'll drive it home safe." She stretched out her hand, not looking at me, her eyes pinned to my boyfriend.

"No!"

"You want me outta here or not?"

"You do realize I'm standing in front of my ride, and I can go and leave you here in a sec?"

"Don't be a dick. I came with you this morning. How am I supposed to go home now?"

"Fine," I growled, my hand already in my pocket. "But I swear if you do as much as scratch it..."

"Stop worrying." She snatched the keys out of my grip and jumped to peck Dusty on the cheek.

My jaw dropped, and he chuckled. "Bye, Ash."

She leaned into me, tilting her head up to reach my ear, and I contemplated pinching her little nose. "Don't be selfish. Think about what I told you in class."

"Fuck you." I raised my foot to kick her butt, but she had already dashed away, giggling.

"She's so cute," Dusty said.

My eyes narrowed at him. "Seriously?"

"What, she's not cute?"

"She is, but only I can say it. When someone *else* does, he's going to be whipped very hard tonight."

A sparkle lit his eyes as he pressed me into him. Into the throbbing erection in his jeans. "Yes, please." His warm breaths danced on my neck, then inside my mouth.

Hot waves of need engulfed me. His hair fell onto his wide shoulders, grazing his cut. My stare roamed the tattooed muscles strained under his white T-shirt, and my hands slid under and down to his back. His ass. Pictures of me spanking these firm cheeks as he…

The sound of my breathing snapped me out of the dirty thoughts and into awareness. "Fuck." I drew back as I realized people were staring. At us. At him.

He pulled me back in without a care in the world, his kisses wet on my neck. If it were for him, he would take me right here right now. I chuckled nervously. "Dusty, we're at school. C'mon, let's get out of here."

He planted a few more kisses down to my throat and collarbones, then a deep one on my lips. "Fine."

His gaze, smoldering but intimidating, shooed the peeping crowds as he opened the studded trunk locked on the bike and handed me a helmet. There was something about Dusty that exuded confidence, but at the same time, he was menacing to strangers. Maybe it was his size or the patch on his cut.

The Night Skulls. My eternal enemy.

He took his helmet and gloves off the handle and put them on. "Hop on."

We flew around the curves of the winding road leading to the coast. I held on tightly, my arms wrapped around his waist. The Harley vibrated loudly between my thighs as I wrapped them around his narrow hips. Heat radiated from his body, and my tight grip kept slipping under his clothes, giving me a chance to feel his rippling muscles.

I was used to riding by now, but with Dusty, it was a different experience. Thrilling. The feeling of the open air rushing past me. The rebelliousness of throwing caution to the wind. The true meaning of letting go.

As we rounded a particularly tight curve, I clutched him even tighter. He reached back, his glove-wrapped hand patting my thigh as if saying, "I got you. Trust me."

And I did. Against all logic. How could I trust him? A Night Skull? Roar's offspring? The new leader of the goddamn gang who killed my sister?

How could I love him this much?

It'd been months since we decided to put the past behind us and become together. Still, I was shocked those feelings were getting through, past all the fear and uncertainty. Past all the despair and the darkness we'd been through.

It was freeing, yet it scared me to the very depths of my soul. My arms tightened around him more as the bike sliced through the wind.

He parked the bike next to a steep flight of stairs that led down to the beach below. We left our helmets on the bike, and he grabbed my hand, intertwining his fingers in mine, as we climbed down.

My boots sank into the sand with each step towards the water. Pink and purple streaks lay over a deep, indigo background. The ocean waves crashed onto the beach, sliding along the slick, undulated sand, and then slinking back into the water.

Dangerously strong. Unstoppable. Like the way we felt for each other.

I turned around and melted into his arms, burying my face in his chest. His huge biceps encircled me, and I felt tiny in his embrace. Safe.

"You're not okay," he said. "What's going on?"

I breathed in deeply, inhaling his scent—the fucking leather—mixed with the saltiness of the ocean air. My body reacted in ways completely in contrast with my brain. "I just miss you."

He broke our hug and sat down on the sand, pulling me down to his lap. I straddled him, and his arms folded around my back.

"I missed you, too, sweetheart. But this isn't what's troubling you." He traced the sunken lines under my eyes. "You've been having those nightmares again?"

My lips pursed as I nodded. "The only time I don't get them is when I'm sleeping in your arms."

"You know there's nothing I want more than to sleep and wake up with you next to me."

Me, too. But the direction he was steering the conversation wasn't something I liked to deal with at the moment. "How long are you staying?"

"Enough to celebrate *Halloween Bloody Valentine's Day* and the weekend after."

I grinned. Not only did he remember our nerdy party, but he was going to stay with me for whole five days.

He gazed at me. "I can stay longer if you'd like."

"Sure. Stay as long as you can."

"You know what I mean."

What he implied was loud and clear, but I really didn't want to go there.

"It's not impossible, Cammie," he pressed.

"We've had this conversation a million times already."

"So what's one more time?"

Persistent son of a bitch. I should just get up and close the subject, but my feet wouldn't move and my hands refused to stop feeling him up. Why was I glued to his lap, adjusting myself to feel more of the erection swelling in his jeans by the second?

He took my hand and kissed it. "Talk to me, sweetheart. You still have concerns about the club?"

I blinked, nudging myself out of the spell he put me under. "That's an interesting word. The Night Skulls is a club now?"

His lips twisted, and his gaze drifted to the waves.

"Listen, Dusty. I know that you have to stay with the gang to protect your mother. What you do with them is your business alone, and I'd never ask you to leave."

"Mama doesn't need protection anymore. Maybe in the beginning, yes, but that was months ago. Everything is settled now. Roar is long forgotten, and no one dares cross me or her."

Forgotten to them but not to me. It didn't matter that he was dead. Everything that piece of shit did to me and my family haunted me.

Literally scarred me for life. "Can we just postpone this talk?"

"For how long? I'm tired of driving two hours back and forth only to see you for a few days every month."

"It's four hours not two."

"Not on my bike, and don't change the subject. I told you I'd leave and come here with you. I don't understand why you keep saying no."

"Well…"

"Well what, Cammie? Why don't you want me here?"

"Because I'm scared." The words fell out of my mouth. I immediately regretted them.

He stared at me, surprised and concerned at the same time. "Of what, baby?"

I finally untangled my legs off him and rose to my feet. "I really don't want to talk about this."

He got up, too, and cupped my face with his hands. "You know I'm not my father, Cammie."

"I know, and I'm sure you'd be better off here away from Rosewood and the gang and the dirty business you run. At least, I won't worry about you the whole fucking time, wondering if you're alive or not. But…"

"But what?"

I swallowed. "What are you going to do here, Dusty? Sit around and wait for me to finish class?" My shoulder lifted in resignation. "You're going to miss your old life, and soon you'll know I'm not enough for you. You'll hate me for everything." Here. I said it. I finally confessed to my biggest fear.

"Not enough for me? Hate you? Where's this shit coming from?"

"*This shit* is the truth."

He laughed. "Geez, baby."

I took his hands off my face. "Why are you laughing?"

"'Cause I thought the reason behind this whole bull was that you liked some fancy-ass college boy, and you were having second thoughts about us. I didn't know it was…" He laughed again.

I kicked at the sand. "It's not funny."

"Yes, it is." He held me tightly, and I could feel his searing heat and the bulge in his jeans on me. "I love you, Cammie, and I'll never feel anything but love for you."

"Dusty…"

His lips silenced me. Soothed me.

He rested his forehead on mine, tucking my ruffled hair behind my ears. "We'll work something out. I'll find something to do, not club related, while you finish your school. Then we'll take it from there. Just give me a couple of weeks to arrange for the whole thing."

"What about the Lanzas?"

"Don't worry about it. I'll deal with them. I won't let anything stand between us, baby."

Again, I found myself under his spell. When I was listening to his heartbeat, wrapped in his embrace like this, and he looked at me with his caring eyes, the intensity of his unwavering attention dissolved every ounce of my distress.

Every move he made was a distraction. Every gesture stopped my racing brain in its tracks. *Relax*, it said. *Everything is going to be just fine.*

"Dusty, I don't want to change you into someone you're not." That was all the resistance left in me.

"And I want to be the man you deserve."

CHAPTER 33

DUSTY

What she'd said at the beach was ridiculous. I was the one scared shitless she'd wake up one day hating me and leave.

If it weren't for the shit we went through together last year, a woman like Cammie never would have chosen to be with a guy like me. A smart, beautiful, sexy as fuck engineer and a biker who barely graduated high school. The daughter of a war hero and the son of a rapist murderer. What were the odds of us lasting a week, let alone months?

But we did.

We didn't see each other every day or lived in the same city. I'd been in constant worry she'd meet someone else, and she'd been worrying I might wind up killed. Still, we'd made it this far. And I intended to stretch this as far as I could.

Until the very end. I had no choice. Cammie had sliced my heart open and tattooed her name in there. She was the only girl for me, and I meant every word I'd told her.

I wouldn't just leave the MC and move here to be with her. I would do anything, change into anything, that made me the man she deserved.

"Dusty." Her voice streamed from the bathroom.

Chills of excitement ran through me as I looked at the bathroom door. She'd come out any second now, wearing the first of my early Valentine's gifts to her.

"You ready, baby?" she asked, and the doorknob clicked.

Naked, sprawled on the bed, hands and feet cuffed, I felt the thrill of losing control and the pain about to tear me when I'd see her in that corset and wouldn't be able to touch her.

"Yes, sweetheart. Please come out," I said, my cock already sticking up.

The lights from the bathroom spilled into the dim hotel room, and she stepped outside. My jaw dropped. My stare glued to her tits hanging out, totally naked, from the leather underbust corset tied behind her neck.

Out of instinct, I tried to get out of the bed, pictures of my mouth and my hands all over her perfect tits taking over me. Then the regret hit hard as I remembered I couldn't move. I was glad, though. I wouldn't have been able to stay in sub mode if I were free when she looked like this.

My tongue darted out, licking my lips as I took my time ogling her nipples before I noticed the rest of the outfit. My eyes dipped to the sweet V of her pussy covered in black lace.

Wait a sec... Are these cutout panties?

I strained my neck to check the crack I thought I saw. Yup. Holy fuck. I only got her the corset, which was more of a selfish gift on my side, but the panties were her addition.

My heart banged against my chest, my whole body burning up, and she hadn't even come near me yet.

She stood there with a confident smirk on her face and a sparkle of satisfaction in her eyes all the time I was watching her. She wasn't fidgeting or hiding anything. Her posture said, "Look at me. Admire my beauty while I take your breath away."

In bed, Cammie was not the vulnerable, traumatized girl that needed my protection and reassurance. She was a woman with a twisted persona and wicked desires that made a guy like me willingly get down on his knees and ask for mercy.

She dominated me in the most beautiful way ever.

I loved both versions. The Cammie I wanted to protect, and the Cammie I was dying to submit to.

"Please come here, sweetheart," I begged.

"I'm not your sweetheart right now." She waved the riding crop in her hand menacingly, the perfect tool to complement her outfit.

"Yes, Mistress. I'm sorry."

She teased the sole of my foot with the crop tip and then gave it a light hit before she approached me. The crop slid up as she moved, and my cock throbbed with anticipation and excitement.

Her lips pressed on mine. Then she cropped me on the thigh. It didn't hurt, but I groaned a little. I knew she liked it when I did. She did it again, the kiss then the crop, many times. Each time a different area. A kiss on the neck and a crop on the foot. A kiss on the stomach and a crop on the side. A foreplay designed to drive me insane in the slowest, most sensual way.

"Please, baby—" I groaned for real as her crop on my inner thigh interrupted me. It was a strong hit this time. "Sorry, Mistress. Just please get on the bed. I really need to touch you."

A playful smirk curved up her mouth as she climbed on top of me. Her tit brushed against my face, almost in my mouth range, when she adjusted herself on my naked body.

Another calculated tease that drove a stream of pre-cum out of my cock. I tugged at the cuffs again, desperate to taste her. When I couldn't, I stared at her hard nipples. "Please."

She bent forward and let her tits slide down my chest with their jutted nipples, scorching me with need. My eyes rolled back. My body lifted on its own, pressing into every part of her as hard as possible.

Her kiss devoured me one more time before the crop landed on my cock. I moaned in her mouth, my body convulsing in pain. She wrapped her fist around my shaft. Instantly, the pain turned into pleasure with her strokes.

Then she leaned into me, setting the crop aside. Both her hands plunged in my hair, pulling my head to her chest. I buried my face between her tits, smelling and licking, until she ordered me to suckle her.

I did as I was told, eagerly, gladly. With each circle and flick of my tongue over her nipples, her juices moistened my stomach through the cutout panties. As her desire dripped on my skin,

I grew even hungrier for her. Her eyes smoldered with a kind of fire I was well aware of now. The kind of wicked passion I craved when she enjoyed herself, immersed deeper into domme mode. It meant one thing. Foreplay was over.

She yanked at my hair, pushing my head away from her. Then her hands wrapped tightly around my neck and cock.

The squeezes, though painful, wound me up in hot arousal. My breaths and groans stopped short in my chest, but my cock grew longer. I stared at her, the wildness in her eyes, my face burning, my head pulsing, and I'd never wanted her more.

It was crazy. It was dangerous. It was painful. But it was so fucking hot.

As my eyes watered, she released my neck but not my erection. I gasped in as much air as I could before her fingers pressed on my throat again.

I was choking, and her juices were flowing. If she gave me a couple of strokes, I'd come in her hands. Even one stroke would do. This was how much aroused she'd made me with her dominant moves.

"Do you want to come?" she asked as if she heard my thoughts.

"Yes, Mistress," I choked. "But only if you'd let me."

She smiled and shook her head, both her hands off me. "Not just yet."

I winced, catching my breath. "Please?"

"You want to come before your mistress? How can that be?" she asked with her sexy rasp that fueled my desire painfully.

"Shame on me. I must be punished really hard."

Her giggle filled the room. "You love to be punished, don't you?"

"Oh, fuck yes."

"How about this for punishment?" She rose to her knees, and her hand tangled in my hair. The other hand went down to her panties, and then she made an inverted V with her index and middle fingers, spreading the cut, exposing her pink opening.

I mumbled some incoherent shit, too lost in that beauty to form words. Suddenly, I found my nose, mouth and chin dipped in her pussy.

Fuck me. That smell. Those delicious juices. This was not punishment. Even if I choked on Cammie's pussy, this was heaven.

She buried me deep inside her, and all I could breathe was the smell of her sex. Her moans flared as I licked her, ate her, fucked her with my tongue.

She pulled my hair harder, but my tongue went inside her deeper. I wished it'd been my cock in her pussy not just my tongue. I wanted to thrust away every need that had been nagging me every day I was away from her.

"I love you," I whispered inside her.

She never said it back, but I didn't care. I knew she wanted me, and that was enough for now. I said it for the both of us until I earned her love. I said it again as I drank her, and she clenched around my tongue.

She yanked my head off her and narrowed her eyes at me. "You look so fucking hot with my juices on your lips and chin like that."

Glancing up into her eyes, I licked my lips, savoring her taste.

"Oh God, Dusty." She scooted back and guided my cock inside her pussy.

"Fuuuuck." My eyes closed as she eased down, taking it all in.

I was already close to the edge, and when she bounced I summoned all my willpower not to come right away.

"You're doing so well, baby," she said as if she sensed my struggle. We moved together, our pelvises grinding against each other. She was clenching and screaming so hard I had no strength left to resist exploding inside her.

"Cammie. Oh, Cammie, I can't hold back."

"No, baby. Not just yet. You're my good boy, and you can hold back. I'm so close." She bounced harder, faster. "That's it. You're doing so well. That's fucking it."

I snapped my eyes shut as her pussy, literally, squeezed my cock, shattering all my hopes to obey her. "Fuck. Fuck! I'm so sorry!"

How was I supposed not to come? With all her beauty and dominant moves and unbelievable body. And that fucking wet pussy. A man could only take so much.

My cum shot in abundance inside her as I prepared myself for whatever punishment she had for me. I didn't mind if she'd torture me all night. The kind of pleasure I had right now was worth it.

Luckily, exploding inside her drove her own orgasm. She cried out my name, her lips a beautiful O, her face as she came the most beautiful sight I'd ever seen.

After a night of making love to her like a sub and like a man, Cammie fell asleep like a baby. For that I was grateful. She'd suffered a lot, and even after all this time, the demons my fucking father had left messing with her head didn't let her rest.

I showered and dressed quietly. My piece in the gun pocket. My dagger into its leather case on my left hip. My second knife into my black leather harnessed biker boots.

I took one last look at my girl in bed, sleeping with nothing covering her but the pale moonlight streaming from the window. Any normal man would not be about to ride a dangerous machine and roar into the night to meet up with bikers and mobsters to plan the future of one of the most infamous MCs in the state.

The Night Skulls didn't do normal, though. We were the rejects of society that breathed chaos. The very definition of rebellion. A gang of misfit criminals. Globally notorious. Dangerous. Powerful. And in one night I became the president of that mess I'd tried so hard to leave behind.

When my father died—when I killed him and my mother took the blame to save my ass—he left an empty seat at the head of the table at Rosewood and a death sentence looming over her head. I had to fill that seat. To save Mama. To pacify the angry men who felt threatened after Roar was no longer there to protect them or their business. To keep the Lanzas on our side and keep the club business going. And for that, I had to do things I'd never be proud of.

But…to be honest…I liked some of it.

If it weren't for Cammie, the moments I stole to be in her arms, to regain my sanity and remind myself who I really was, I'd lose myself to The

Night Skulls. I might never tell her that, but the power, the darkness…were addicting.

I had to get out of Rosewood as fast as I could. I needed to be here with her, where we both silenced each other's demons. For that to happen, to keep my promise to her, I had to interrupt our time together and call for a meet here in SLO.

A couple more weeks of hustling. That was all. And then I'd be all hers.

CHAPTER 34

CAMERON

Dusty thought I didn't hear him leave, just like he was thinking I was still asleep when he tiptoed into the room and slid back under the sheets next to me now.

He'd been gone for hours. The chirping outside the window and the sun heating my back confirmed it. I was angry. Worried. Intending to fight. But his arms wrapped around me—thick, strong and safe—and I decided it could wait. I pressed my body backwards into him, letting him know I was awake.

"Shit. Did I wake you?" His mouth on my neck sent a beautiful shiver down my core. "Sorry, baby. Go back to sleep."

I moaned in protest, reaching back to grip his naked cock. Dusty slept in the nude, and I loved that about him as much as I loved how his cock stiffened in my fist with one single touch.

He moaned, too. Then his kisses trailed down my neck and along the back of my shoulder. I stroked him up and down until he was groaning through the kisses. More than ready for him, I lifted my thigh, and he slid into me.

We pressed into each other, pushing, pulling, fulfilling the need that never ended every morning we woke up together. Even after a long night of hot, dirty sex.

The way he filled me never stopped to amaze me, and my body responded to him in ways I'd never experienced with anyone else. He knew when to move slowly, seductively, pulling me out of my head and into the pleasures of my body, and when to wildly take me with the full force of his masculinity. When to submit. When to take control.

My moans turned into screams, and his own need took over as he hammered into me. I opened my eyes to watch him, the ecstasy on his face after those last few moments of focused, savage desire. It made me feel needed. Wanted.

Loved.

The lustful, passionate thrusting brought us both over the edge. His cock spilled into me as we came almost together in a chorus of screams that made me thankful we weren't at my apartment with Ashley listening in the other room.

He pulled me in for a kiss on the lips, but I shied away. "Morning breath."

"I don't give a shit." He scorched me with a kiss that made me want him again even if I'd just climaxed. I laughed and shook my head.

"What?" He smiled, panting, resting his head on the pillow.

"I was so mad at you for sneaking out in the middle of the night like that, and now all I want is to have you inside me. Again."

He kissed me one more time. "First, I'm sorry I left. I thought you were sleeping and didn't want to wake you. Second…" His fingers crawled near my pussy. "There's nowhere I'd rather be than inside you."

I was wet with his seed and my desire, and his thumb, now teasing my burning clit, wasn't helping me stay focused on finding out where he'd gone. "Dusty…"

Sweat glistened on his face and muscles, making him irresistible. "Just give me a few seconds to recover, and I'll go as many times as you want."

"No," I chuckled. "Stop it. I want to know where you went. I thought I'd have you for myself the whole five days."

"That was the plan, but now I need to shift gears to get everything done in those two weeks."

"And by everything you mean?" I'd never asked about what he did or would do in the gang. But now that he was going to leave, it wouldn't hurt to get some details.

"Sweetheart, you don't have to worry about a thing. Leave it all to me."

His lips were on my nipple as his fingers fluttered between my folds. Not fair. "At least, tell me who you're going to leave The Night Skulls to," I moaned. "Beth?"

Suddenly, he stilled. Then his head lifted from my breast and stared at me. "Every time you call Mama by her real name I'm shocked as if I didn't know she shared it with you. I still can't get past her revealing it to you like that."

"That woman would do anything for you. You, too." That dance they did after Roar's death to save each other, as if they'd rehearsed a thousand times before, yet they'd never even had a chance to discuss it, was mind blowing. "We both know that."

"So you like Mama now?"

I rolled my eyes. "Like?" That woman was a psychopath, and if it weren't for the fact that I was the only one who knew where Dusty had been at that time, she would have probably tortured me a lot worse than Roar had. "She saved my life and yours, for that she'll always have my gratitude and respect."

He cackled. "Fair enough."

"Sure she's no fan of mine either. I mean I'll always be the woman who kidnapped her son."

"Best time of my life." His mouth and fingers returned with a vengeance, blowing my fucking mind.

I bit my lip, shuddering. "Stop distracting me and answer the question." No matter how easy it was to lose myself and melt into Dusty, I needed to know. Besides, if we got started again, we'd never stop, and I had to be in class in a couple of hours.

"No. Not Mama," he mumbled, not leaving my now engorged nipple.

"Seriously?"

He looked up at me, giving me a multiple, quick flicks with his tongue before he released my breast with a pop. "She won't be happy about it, but putting her in command could start an unnecessary riot inside the MC. It sounds sexist, but she's a woman. An ol'lady. The Night Skulls is always run by men, patched members. Not to mention the other chapters. Even if we made an exception, after what they think she did to Roar, they wouldn't be very pleased."

I took a moment to let it all sink in. "So who's going to be the next Night Skulls' President?"

CHAPTER 35

CAMERON

In the next couple days, I learned Dusty hadn't decided yet which Night Skull he was going to nominate as his successor. That was why he had that meeting with the Lanzas and his VP. Rush.

I was shocked to know Dusty kept Roar's VP as his. Was it another demand from Cosimo Lanza or did Dusty approve of the position himself?

"Why on earth did you make him your VP?" I'd kept myself out of anything MC related, but I was unable to keep my mouth shut any longer.

Dusty ran a hand through his wet hair, nothing covering his body but a towel around his waist. "What do you mean?"

"That man, Rush, must have ulterior motives to behave the way he did back then. Turning down the presidency because the Lanzas said so? And how quickly he was on Mama's side? Something is off. Besides, he was *Roar's* VP. He can't be trusted."

He stared at me for a second. Then a pale smile stretched his lips.

I shrugged. "What?"

"You worry too much, sweetheart. Why don't you leave—"

"Leave it all to you. Yeah, yeah." I waved a dismissive hand as I spun to head into the shower. Tonight was the Halloween early Valentine's. I needed to get ready. The last thing I wanted was a fight.

Besides, he was right. I should leave it all to him. I should stay away from anything Night Skulls like I always did. Couldn't keep my mouth shut for two more weeks? What was I thinking? Why did I have to ask about the new president? Now I was more worried and afraid for Dusty, and those upcoming couple of weeks wouldn't be as easy as I thought they would be.

I started for the bathroom, but his hand on my waist stopped me in my tracks. I looked at him over my shoulder, both his arms folded around me from behind now.

"I know you're worried," he said. "Outside the MC, Rush can't be considered…a good man. But inside, he's one of the best."

I sighed, my jaws tight.

"I know it's hard for you to believe this, but we're brothers, a family. We have a code, Cammie. Breaking it means nothing but a death sentence. Even if he has *ulterior motives*, he can't act upon them."

We. A constant reminder that Dusty was a Night Skull whether he wanted to be in that gang or not. "You turned your back on the MC, Roar and offed him. I don't see you dead."

"I would have been," he said quickly. "If it weren't for Mama…and Rush."

"So you trust this guy enough to make him second in command?"

"It's not just about trust. The Skulls listened to Rush. I needed him on my side if I wanted them to listen to me, too. And knowing he'd never hurt Mama was a plus at the time."

I turned and nestled in his big arms. His logic and the safety of his embrace eased my concerns a bit. But I was scared of the darkness that constantly surrounded him. He was in too deep. It'd ultimately change him, swallow him whole. "I understand. It's just…hard, to know how amazing and caring and good you are and yet you…rule that place. I mean…" Words betrayed me.

"It's just for two more weeks, baby."

"Yes. I'm probably overreacting about this whole thing. You obviously know what you're doing."

He kissed me on the forehead. "Thank you."

His hug was warm and soothing, but I had to break it to get ready. I showered and dried my hair fast. When I got out of the bathroom, my jaw dropped low, practically drooling.

Dusty was in a suit.

A dashing blue suit with a tight white shirt underneath. His hair smoothed to the back and hanged perfectly on his shoulders. Holy smokes.

It wasn't like he didn't rock that biker, leathery look, but this was a whole new level of hotness I wasn't prepared for.

"What?" He had his crooked smile on.

Like he needed that too.

I blinked, laughing. "I don't think we're going to make it to dinner."

He chuckled, his thumb pointing to the bed. "Maybe when you see your new dress, you'll change your mind."

What new dress? I already had a red dress I intended to wear for tonight. I dragged my gaze from his mesmerizing figure and glanced over at the bed. A red satin dress spread across the brown flowered bedspread. A pair of red pumps. And a…jewelry box.

My jaw fell open again. "Oh my God, baby."

He took my hand and printed a kiss on the palm. "Don't just stand there. Go try everything on."

I took off the bathrobe, already in my underwear, and slipped on the dress. The fabric felt amazing on my skin. It hugged my curves a little too tight and was a little shorter than anything I'd choose on my own, but it was sexy as hell. The sudden swell in Dusty's dress pants confirmed it.

As I put on the pumps, he frowned all of a sudden, biting his lip. "I changed my mind. There's no way I'm gonna let you go out like this."

"Excuse me?"

"Look at you! You're…" He ate me with his stare. "Fucking wow."

A grin spread on my face. "Thank you. You're *fucking wow*, too."

"I'm serious, Cammie. Wear the other dress. You don't want me walking with a hard-on the whole night."

I loved that dress and those shoes. No way I was going to take them off. "I don't mind." I winked, secretly thankful for being a woman that could easily hide her arousal with a bra.

"What about every other fucker at the party? You want them to have hard-ons over you, too?"

"Who cares about their little dicks?" I felt him up over the pants, biting my lip. "When I have you…"

His eyes lifted to the ceiling. "You love to torture me."

"Duh." I spanked his ass. Good Heavens.

He finally laughed. "Fine. Aren't you gonna open the box?"

Goosebumps spread on my arms as he grabbed the velvet thing and held it to my face. I opened it, and my brows shot up as I took in the blinding sparkle inside. "Dusty… This's… I'm speechless."

"You like them?"

"Like them?" I couldn't take my eyes off the necklace with the heart pendant rimmed with bling and little rubies or the set of matching earrings. "Are these…silver?" I couldn't say what I really suspected. These were definitely not silver.

"Uh…no. They're white gold, but the little diamonds and rubies are real."

My head jerked up. "This is way too much. How can you affor—" I chopped off my question. "Never mind. I can't accept them."

"What? No, sweetheart. You never let me buy you anything 'cause you're iffy about Skulls' money, I get that. But I swear to you I bought those with clean money."

"Yeah?"

"Yes, baby."

A smile triumphed on my face. Discovering he was making the effort to make me happy, to reassure me all the time, made me feel so lucky. No guy did that for me before that I started to think men didn't do that at all.

I was wrong. Dusty did. My Dusty.

"I love you," I murmured, reflexively.

He stilled for a moment, and I didn't dare lift my gaze to him. "What did you just say?"

I said. I finally said it. It was real and raw and spontaneous, but it scared the fuck out of me.

He lifted my chin with his finger and made me look at him. "I've been waiting to hear it from you for months. When you finally say it, it won't be shy, reluctant or hushed. You have to look me in the eye and say it with the confidence of that strong girl you are, the one that defied danger to avenge her sister and brought me to my knees with her kindness before power."

His words touched me so beautifully my eyes threatened to ruin my makeup. I gazed at him, drawing in on that confidence I discovered because of him, for him, and smiled. "I love you, Dusty."

He pulled me in a tight embrace, and then he rested his forehead on mine while our lips caressed. "I love you, too. Always."

My smile grew bigger, and he unhooked the chain lock and went behind me to put the necklace on me. Then the earrings. We both looked in the dresser mirror, and I thought we looked amazing together.

"I've never seen anything more beautiful than you." He offered me his arm. "Shall we?"

CHAPTER 36

DUSTY

The limo was waiting outside the hotel entrance as we exited. Riding the bike with Cammie dressed like that was fucking impossible. Everybody was looking at her. Even the driver stole a few glances at her curves as he opened the door for us.

My blood simmered in my veins. It wasn't like me to get jealous. I grew up in a place where every pussy was for everybody to share. But with Cammie, everything was different. I was different.

She was my girl, my ol'lady. If we were in Rosewood, no one would dare look at her. Here…I had to be a *decent* guy and play by the rules. Fancy fucking college town rules. Soon, it was gonna be my town, too. I had to get used to it.

"Wow. It's like we're going to Prom." She giggled, climbing into the limo.

I swallowed my anger as I saw how happy she was. "Did you like going to yours?"

"Uh, I've never gone to mine. Have you?"

"Hell no. Not my thing." I settled next to her as the driver shut the door. "Why did you miss yours?"

She frowned, her eyes dark abruptly. "I… Sylvia, you know my *mother* had just left us then, and…my fucking boyfriend at the time was… He tried to… You know what? This is not the right time for this story." Her fingers twined with mine, squeezing.

Murderous thoughts banged my skull at the idea of some douche hurting Cammie in any way, and the way she was talking made me think of the worst. Fury raptured inside me and forced me to not let the conversation slide. "Give me a name."

"What?"

"The name of that fucker. What did he try to do?"

She blinked. "Dusty, chill. That was years ago. He was just a boy."

"Cameron!" Pressure pounded my head. "Did he touch you?"

Her frown deepened. "Nothing happened," she said firmly. "I broke up with him, and after graduation I never saw him again. End of story. Now, I'd like to enjoy this weird ass nerdy Valentine's with you. Can we not ruin tonight with this testosterone frenzy please?"

I'd been planning this night for weeks for her. The surprise. The money for the gifts. The hotel. The party. Everything. The last thing I wanted was to fuck it up. I couldn't help feeling all that rage when I found out someone, anyone, had hurt her, though. "I'll drop it now, but you have to promise to tell me all about it later."

She rolled her eyes. "Fine."

I squeezed her hand gently and then kissed it. She gave me a small smile, and the car stopped. Looking through the tinted window, I realized we arrived at the club.

Her eyes lit again as she saw the blue neon lights of the Tempo. "I love this place."

The limo stopped, and the driver opened the door for us. "Wait, why are we here?" she asked. "That's not where they booked the party."

Another surprise for my baby girl. The queen that owned my heart. "I thought we could have our own party first."

"Shut up. For real?"

"Yup."

We climbed out of the limo, and she leaned into me, resting her head on my shoulder. "This is my favorite place in town. How did you know?"

"I have connections."

"Of course. Ash." She glanced up at me, her eyes wide. "Did she know you were coming to the party all along?"

"Nah. She just helped me out when I asked her. She's the one who told me you liked rubies, too," I said. "You know it's a shame I had to know these things from your friend. I figured out I don't know so much about you after all this time."

She chuckled and stuck her hand out. "Cameron Delaney. Cal Poly. Final year. I study engineering. Nice to meet you."

I laughed and took her hand in mine, shaking my head, leading her inside the club. After I gave my name to the hostess, she guided us to our reserved booth, especially decorated for Valentine's unlike the rest that were turned spooky for Halloween.

"Oh my God." Cammie's jaw hung low. "Dusty…you're amazing."

"Anything for you, sweetheart."

Cammie moved her head with the music as her eyes scanned the food items. "They have a new list for tonight. Wait a minute." She stared at me. "This is a special menu, and it's not Halloween. Did you ask them to do that, too?"

"You sounded pretty psyched about Valentine's. I wanted to give you the whole experience."

She tangled her fingers in my hair and kissed me hard. "I really love you."

"I love you, too. I'm so lucky you're mine."

"I'm so lucky I'm yours." She put her fingers among mine and squeezed my hand. Then she tucked her hair behind her ear. "The Strip Me Down sounds delicious."

"You got it."

We laughed together, and then I kissed her cherry lips. Her hand touched my knee and glided up my thigh and back to my ass. This wild desire she ignited in me every time she touched me was impossible to contain. My lips mashed against hers with raw passion. The force of my grip on her body made her moan. My cock strained against my pants.

A little cough came from behind, jolting me out the intensity of the moment. "Excuse me, sir?"

Cammie pulled away, pressing her swollen lips as she looked at the woman who dared interrupt us and the flowers in her hands.

"Happy Valentine's Day, Miss," the waitress said, handing Cammie the bouquet.

Shit. I'd totally forgotten about those. I'd called the club and arranged for a large bouquet of red and white roses, a box of chocolate and champagne, and asked them to serve them when we arrived.

"Wow. They're very beautiful. Thank you." Cammie took the bouquet, staring at me. "Never thought *you* would get me flowers."

"I love you enough to do that horrible, ugly flower buying thing," I mocked. Maybe I wasn't the flower-buying type, but I'd do anything to make her happy. To deserve her. Lost in her eyes, I licked my lips. Her taste lingered there.

"Would you like your chocolate and champagne served now?" the waitress asked, yanking me out of the moment again.

"Yes," I answered, a little too loudly. "And take our order, too. One Strip Me Down and one Bite Me."

She bit her thin lips on a smile, her boney cheeks flushed, her stare *stripping me down*. "Right away, sir."

But she remained still by the table, blatantly looking at my hard dick.

"That will be all, thank you," Cammie yelled over the music.

The waitress blinked, blushing. "Sure. I'll be right back with your order." She flipped her blond hair as she spun and left with an exaggerated strut that swayed her skinny ass in that snug, glittery black dress.

"You like her?" Cammie asked, placing the bouquet on the table.

My brows hooked as I looked at her sideways. "What?"

She stared me down, moon-eyed. "She likes you, too, you know?"

I couldn't resist snickering.

"You think this is funny?"

"Yeah."

She glared at me, her jaws tight.

"Baby, you're so hot when you're jealous, but how could you be jealous of someone like her?" I asked, amused, not waiting for an answer.

She crossed her arms over her chest, giving me a great view of her rack. "You were checking her out."

"I wasn't. I was like *what the fuck, can't she see the gorgeous girl I'm with?*" I leaned in, my gaze locked with hers, hoping she would see the sincerity in my eyes.

Her tits rose as she inhaled, and a hint of smile tampered with her 'I'm mad at you' face. "Whatever."

"You gotta loosen up a little." My palm rested on her bare knee and quickly went up along her inner thigh and onto her panties. Then I slipped underneath the lace. "I know how to help you with that."

She flinched with a gasp. "You crazy?"

I cupped her whole pussy at first, and then teased the lips with my fingertips, smirking. "Take off my hand, if you don't like it."

She opened her mouth then closed it with a shy smile. "That bitch is going to be here with the champagne any time."

"So?" My thumb pressed her clit.

She leaned forward, her elbows on the table, her eyes darting around, her breaths ragged. "She'll see."

I slid one finger inside her wetness. The heat radiating from her sent my cock twitching. Big twitches. "Who cares?"

She licked her lips, shifting in her seat. "You're so naughty."

"I think you know that by now," I whispered as I leaned in for another kiss. "And you love to punish me for it as much as I do."

Her lips crushed mine before I reached them, as if she was the one overwhelmed with need, not me. I slipped another finger in her pussy, my thumb still on her clit. Her moans against my mouth drove my own. I wanted to throw her over my shoulder caveman-style, run back to the hotel and...

"Your champagne, sir."

Cammie drew back as the waitress interrupted us. Again. I didn't remove my hand or fingers dipped in my girlfriend's juices, though. I didn't even bother to look at the waitress. My eyes remained on Cammie, who was flushed, hands shaking a little as she took the red, heart-shaped chocolate box from her.

"Thanks." She set it aside on the table as the champagne bottle popped behind me.

I sank my fingers deeper and then pulled them slowly. In and out. In and out. She gave me a warning stare, the back of her hand covering her mouth. That didn't stop me. It only made me move faster.

"Jesus... Could you... Could you please hurry?" Cammie waved at the waitress, and I stifled a laugh.

As soon as Cammie's glass was poured, she gulped on it. "Umm… Oh God…this is…very good champagne."

I cackled and finally glanced at the waitress. "Tell the kitchen to speed up our orders. Looks like we're not staying as long as planned."

The blonde was practically straining her neck, her eyes moving back and forth to get a good view of my pants and what I was doing under the table, but the way I was sitting obscured the whole thing.

"Did you hear me, doll?" I asked.

"Yes, sir. Of course." She took a ridiculous amount of time pouring my glass. Then she left with the same exaggerated ass-wiggle.

I looked back at Cammie. She wasn't jealous or mad, her eyes full of nothing but smoldering lust. My fingers fluttered inside her, and then moved in circular motions. She drew in and touched my cock, and then sucked in a breath between her teeth. "Fuck, Dusty. You're so hard."

I nodded. Her flowing juices around my fingers and her fist pressing tight around my erection poured fuel on my own desire. Approaching her ear, I could smell her sweet perfume mixed with the hot scent of her soaked pussy. "I wish it was my cock inside you while your hand choked my neck and you gagged me with your tit."

With this, she buried her head in my shoulder, moaning, her pussy crushing my fingers as she came.

Gently, I pulled out of her. Then I inhaled my sticky fingers, closing my eyes with a groan, my erection aching in my pants.

"You want to get out of here, right?" she rasped.

"My cock does, but it can wait." The last part was a lie. I couldn't wait at all. And this place, even that I loved upscale night clubs, was too girly for my taste. Making her happy was on the top of my list, though.

"I don't mind. That blonde bitch would probably spit in our food anyway. So, what do you say? Have one dance and finish that champagne back at the hotel?"

"What about the early Bloody Valentine's?"

"Fuck it. What you've done for me tonight is incredible. I don't need or want anything else but you dancing with me and then buried deep inside me."

I grinned. "Sure. Just give me a moment for this hard-on to go down a notch for the dance."

She looked, giggling. "I think you'll need more than a moment."

Nodding in agreement, I downed my glass. This sissy French thing wasn't my drink, but I was desperate for any form of alcohol to cool off.

"Hey, Cameron." A guy in a brown suit stopped at our booth, holding a drink with a straw in it.

Seriously? What guy does that? And who the fuck was that dude anyway?

"Samuel, hi," Cammie greeted. She gestured between me and him. "This's my boyfriend, Dusty. Samuel and I go to school together."

"Hey." He nodded at me, sizing me up. "You're a very lucky guy."

I picked something nasty in his tone. Had this ass tried something with my ol'lady before? The urge to punch his crooked nose flat tempted me. So much. "Yeah, I was just telling her that. Luckier than any guy in this whole town will ever be."

My phone vibrated in my pocket, distracting me for a second. I saw Mama's name blinking on the screen and decided to let the punching slide for now. His ass wouldn't stand a chance anyway. Even though he was around six feet and had broad chest and shoulders, when he saw my size compared to his if I just got up, he'd piss his pants.

Cammie touched my arm, smiling, as if she'd sensed my anger and was asking me to calm down. "You need to take this?"

I glared at the douche and shoved the phone back in my pocket. "Nah. It can wait."

"So what are you doing here? Shouldn't you be at the party with your date?" she asked him.

"Uh…I'm here with a bunch of guys from Mechanics, you know…warming up." He pointed at the bar with his thumb. "Valentine's is the perfect day for hookups." His eyes shifted to me. "It's not really for couples anymore."

I gritted my teeth, and if it wasn't for the non-stopping vibration of my phone and Cammie, I would be enjoying rearranging his face right now.

"Well, good luck then," she said and looked at me. "Care for that dance now?"

I gave the asshole another pointed look. "Sure."

On the dance floor, I could see him with his friends as they sipped on their ball busting drinks at the bar. His eyes lingered on her every two seconds. Then every time he realized I was watching him, he looked away. The only thing that was keeping me from doing something really stupid was how happy Cammie was swaying in my arms.

However, the asshole never stopped stealing glances at my ol'lady, and my phone didn't stop shaking. As much as I tried to ignore everything and enjoy the night with my girl, the universe was standing against it.

I got my phone out. Five missed calls and thirteen texts. All from Mama, swearing, demanding me to pick up urgently.

What the fuck was going on?

CHAPTER 37

CAMERON

When I saw it was Beth calling, I could tell something was wrong. She never called when he was here. "Just answer, baby."

His eyes narrowed at the guys at the bar for a second, and he seemed to be struggling with something. "Don't wanna leave you here alone."

"Dusty, c'mon. They won't eat me." I pointed at his phone. "It hasn't stopped ringing. Must be important."

"Fine." He rubbed my arm and got a big wad of cash from the inner pocket of his suit jacket.

At least a thousand dollars. "Can you take care of the check so we can go right after?"

"Sure."

"Thank you." He placed the money in my hand and darted outside, his phone already on his ear.

I got off the dance floor and waved for the waitress to get the check. As I headed back to the booth, Samuel blocked my way.

"You serious with that guy?" he drawled, shifting on his feet, off-balanced.

Samuel had asked me out once, and I'd told him I had a boyfriend. We never talked about this again. What the hell was going on with him tonight? Did he not believe me then and now was surprised it was true?

I smirked. "Not that it's any of your business, but yes, dead serious."

"So that's the kinda guy you like? Criminal dropouts that treat girls like their properties?"

"What the... You know what? Never mind. You're wasted. Go fish for that hookup somewhere else." There was no point carrying this conversation.

I tried to move past him, but he grabbed my arm. "How about a little dance till he returns? Maybe you'll change your mind."

My eyes narrowed at his hand and then lifted with the best menacing look I could muster. "Take your filthy hand off my arm now."

"C'mon, Cameron. Just one dance." The back of his hand slid up along my arm. Then I felt his other hand low on my back, almost on my butt.

I shook him off me. "I said no."

He grabbed me again, harder, his grip hurting my flesh. "You will dance with me."

Okay. I'm done playing nice.

CHAPTER 38

DUSTY

"Mama, you all right?" I asked the second I was out of music range.

"No, Dusty, I'm not. Have you lost your mind?"

Worry and rage took over me as I pushed the doors open and exited to the back alley behind the club. "What are you talking about? What happened?"

"What do you mean what happened? You don't know what happened? You're stepping the fuck down!"

I tilted my head back and exhaled a long, heated breath, rolling my eyes, my blood boiling. "You shitting me right now? I thought something happened to you like you got busted or attacked or something. What the hell, Mama?"

"This is way worse! Tell me it's not true."

I will kill that fucker Rush. I told him not to tell anyone just yet.

My hand clenched, and I almost hurled the phone at the reeking Dumpster in front of me. "No, it is true. As far as I remember, I'm President. This's my call and my call alone. Now, if you don't mind I need to get back to my ol'lady."

"You're throwing everything away for that bitch?!"

My eyes squeezed shut. "Mama, don't call her that. Cammie and I are together whether you like it or not."

"She fucking kidnapped you."

"We killed her sister," I seethed in the lowest tone possible. "She could've let me rot, but she didn't. She made sure I'd get out whether she came out of Rosewood dead or alive. And I love her. End of story."

"Dusty—"

"Enough. I'm hanging up."

Shoving the phone back into my pocket, I banged the door open and hurried back inside the club. My stare sought after Cammie immediately. I found her talking to that ass, his fucking hand on her arm.

What the fuck? That piece of shit should know patience wasn't my friend. There was so much I could take.

I elbowed through the crowd, my anger piling up. Then I saw him grabbing her again. *You brought it on yourself, motherfucker.*

How many people had I pushed out of my way to reach Cammie? How many slaps or arm twists had *she* given the piece of shit until my fist sucker punched him? I didn't know. I couldn't see.

It was like I wasn't here anymore, and there was no one around but him and me and the shitty enraging things that happened today. How other men looked at Cammie. What she said about her high school ex. What Mama said. How that fucker thought he could lay a hand on my girl.

Blinded by rage, I dragged him off the floor— he'd fallen flat on his ass from my punch—and kicked him into that alley.

He was talking, but I couldn't hear anything but the breaking of his bones as I smashed his face. Blood splattered all over me, but I didn't stop.

I didn't want to stop.

His left arm was my next victim. I stretched it and twisted it until it snapped. He rolled in pain, crying, but I pinned him down and my punches flew again. The fucker's screams and blubbering fell deaf on my ears. Even the footsteps and the yelling men and screaming women behind me. Every sound was toned down until one scream snapped me out of my own skin. Cammie's scream.

"Dusty! Stop! You'll kill him!"

I looked at her over my shoulder and saw her pale face and the panic in her eyes. The world stopped in its tracks as I realized, for the first time ever, Cameron was terrified of me.

Suddenly, I became aware of the surroundings, the people, the blood. The approaching sirens.

I stood and grabbed the piece of shit by his neck. Then I pressed him to the Dumpster. His eyes were swollen and half-closed, but I knew he could still see me. I leaned to whisper in his ear. "If you ever think about touching my woman again, I'll chop your dick off in your sleep. And if you go yammering to the cops, I'll track you and your family down, and when I find you, it won't be about breaking some bones like tonight. It'll be a lot fucking worse. Graveyard worse. Do you understand?"

He nodded vigorously, sobbing like a little bitch.

"Now, apologize to her." I moved to the side, making space for him to see her, still holding him so he wouldn't fall.

"I'm sorry," he blubbered, blood gushing from his teeth. "I'm so sorry. I'll never touch you again."

"Good bitch. Remember what I said about not breaking your bones next time," I whispered.

"Yes. Yes! I'm sorry."

I let him drop and yanked Cammie by the hand out of the crowd.

CHAPTER 39

DUSTY

We managed to leave before the cops arrived, and silence filled the limo on our way back to the hotel.

The second she stomped into the room, she grabbed her bag and clothes from the closet.

I slammed the door shut and went after her. "What are you doing?"

"Packing. I gotta get out of here," she mumbled.

"What?"

She stuffed her things into the bag. "I need to go back to my place."

"You're not going anywhere."

"Yes, I am."

I snatched everything in her hands and threw it on the floor. "I said you are not going anywhere."

She blinked with the thud her now blood-stained stuff made when it fell. Then she looked up at me, defiantly. "Or what? You'll beat the crap out of me, too?"

My eyes widened. She knew I'd never lay a hand on her. What the fuck? "Cammie, please. This is crazy. Can we talk?"

She bent and picked up the fucking bag, packing again, ignoring me.

A huge wave of tension rumbled inside me. "Fine. I admit I was angry. It's been building up all night. First with how everybody was looking at you in that dress, and then that asshole boyfriend story." And what Mama said, but I couldn't tell Cammie about it now.

She placed the unzipped, half-filled bag on the bed and stumbled, getting me out of her way to reach the dresser.

I held her arm, not letting her pass. "I saw that motherfucker all over you, what was I supposed to do?"

She jerked out of my grip. "Not beat him to death!"

"I was protecting you! It's my fucking job."

"You think a girl like me can't handle herself? Even if I can't, killing the guy is your first resolution of conflict?"

"*Resolution of conflict?* What is this shit?" My hands flew in the air. "I wasn't gonna kill him, I was teaching the fucker a lesson."

"Didn't look like that to me."

"Cammie—"

"My moral compass doesn't exactly point north. I mean I've done some terrible shit. To you." Her eyes rimmed with tears. "That doesn't mean I go kill anyone I don't like."

"Again, I thought I was protecting you, Cameron. It's not what you think."

"Yes, it is. This isn't about any of the shit you said or protection or jealousy. Everywhere we go, girls are ogling you. I get jealous as fuck. I want to rip their eyes out of their cavities and beat the hell out of every girl who flirts with you, but do you see me fucking do it?" she yelled. "This is about you. What you're capable of."

My hands landed on my hips instead of punching a wall. "You're wrong."

"Am I? Well, answer me this. What were you planning on doing if I gave you the name of my high school ex and told you he had abused me in any way?"

I was gonna make him beg for death before I finished him.

Her tears stained her face as she stared at me, waiting for an answer she already knew. "All this time, I was terrified to ask you what kind of things you've been doing for the gang because of this moment." She wiped her face fast. "The moment I find out you kill just because you can."

"Again, not true. But you know as much as I do some fuckers deserve to die. It's a necessity."

"Are you listening to yourself right now?" she whimpered, startled. "Isn't that what Roar used to tell you?"

"I didn't hear you lecturing me when I took my own father's life for you."

Her eyes widened, and then she blinked once. "You blame me for it now? I never asked you to do that for me."

Fuck. I looked down, surprised at my words, too. "I know. Of course, I don't blame you. I'm sorry."

Tears dropped down her face. "I believed you. I lied to myself and chose to believe you when you asked me to stay and told me none of this would ever come between us. I chose to believe you when you kept saying you were not your father, and you ran things differently, but look at you. The next thing I know you'll be kidnapping fifteen-year-old girls and raping them to death."

My skin crawled. "That's not fair. I'd never do that, and you know it."

"Why? Because you're above it? Because it's not as equally horrendous as taking innocent lives?"

"Cammie, sweetheart. I know I overreacted tonight." I reached to hold her but stopped short. I didn't want to get any blood on her. "I'm so sorry. I thought he was hurting you, and I snapped."

She was crying again, throwing more things inside her bag.

"Cameron, please. I promise it won't happen again."

"It doesn't matter."

"What's that supposed to mean?" My stomach tied in a knot by the calm resolution in her tone. "You think the MC is changing me and messing with my head. That's what you mean, right?"

She didn't answer, but I refused to believe she literally meant what she was implying. "Well, it's all gonna be over in two weeks anyway, maybe even earlier. No funny business. No more Night Skulls. We'll start fresh. I'll make it up to you, I swear."

"No." Her rasp was low and cold.

"What do you mean no? What are you… What are you telling me, Cammie?"

She zipped the bag and walked to the door, sniffling. Then she spun and looked at me. "Go back to Rosewood. To your brothers. To your Mama. And stay. It's where you truly belong."

"Fuck this shit!" I took the fucking bag and hurled it against the wall. "I'm not fucking leaving and neither are you."

She stared at me, at my fists that clenched so hard my knuckles were white. Shit. I was scaring her again. I reached for her hand. "Baby—"

She flinched, stepping back. "I'm done lying to myself. You should do the same."

I shook my head, hissing. I needed to touch her, to show her it was still me, the man who would do anything for her, the man who would never hurt her, but she was terrified of me. It was the worst thing I'd ever felt in my life. It fucking paralyzed me.

She grabbed her bag again and faced the door. "The worst part is…I wasn't lying to myself when I fell with love with you."

"Then stay. Do you want me to beg, because I will? I will go on my knees and beg for as long as it takes to make you stay."

Her hand and tears fell on the knob. "Goodbye, Dusty."

I couldn't believe she walked out of that door. I couldn't believe I had to let her because I scared her to the point of no return.

I'd lost myself, and with it I lost the only girl I'd ever loved.

But no. I wouldn't give up. Couldn't. I had to find a way to win her back. She had to know I'd never let her go. She was mine. Whether she liked it or not.

To be continued…

✽✽✽✽✽

Thanks for Reading, Playlist and Part Two!

I hope you've enjoyed the beginning of Dusty and Cammie's story. As you know, this is a duet which means there are many questions yet to be answered. There are so many secrets left to unravel and conflicts to resolve in the next book. Cameron, part two and the conclusion of this duet is ready for you to devour, and I promise a happy ending

Read Cameron now
https://books2read.com/cameronsf
Read Furore and Tirone duet in the same series
https://books2read.com/furore
followed by the sequel Night Skulls Mayhem

If you haven't read Forbidden Cruel Italians Mafia series and anxious to know who the Lanzas are, this is for you:

- **Start The Italians series PREQUEL FREE with The Cruel Italian** https://BookHip.com/RCSXCGR**For Enzio Lanza's book,** read and download <u>The Italian Marriage</u> now
- **For Tino Bellomo's book,** read **The Italian Obsession**
- **For Dom Lanza's book,** download <u>The Italian Dom</u>
- **For Leo Bellomo's book download The Italian Son**

To take a break from dark reads but still get the spice of hot Italian men:

- **Read Mike Gennaro's book** <u>The Italian Heartthrob</u>
- **Read Fabio Zappa's book** <u>The Italian Happy Ever After</u>

Join my Newsletter for extra scenes, free books and updates
Njadelbooks.com

SOUNDTRACK

Listen to the full playlist on Spotify
https://spoti.fi/3R9z0Mm

ALSO BY N.J. ADEL

Contemporary Romance
The Italian Heartthrob
The Italian Happy Ever After
The Italian Marriage
The Italian Obsession
The Italian Dom
The Italian Son

Paranormal Reverse Harem
All the Teacher's Pet Beasts
All the Teacher's Little Belles
All the Teacher's Bad Boys
All the Teacher's Prisoners

Reverse Harem Erotic Romance
Her Royal Harem: Complete Box Set

Dark MC and Mafia Romance
Furore
Tirone
Dusty
Cameron
Night Skulls Mayhem

AUTHOR BIO

N. J. Adel, the author of The Italians, The Night Skulls MC, All the Teacher's Pets, and Her Royal Harem, is a cross genre author. From chocolate to books and book boyfriends, she likes it DARK and SPICY.

Mafia bosses, psycho anti-heroes, bikers, rock stars, dirty Hollywood heartthrobs, supes, smexy guards and men who serve. She loves it all.

She is a loather of cats and thinks they are Satan's pets. She used to teach English by day and write fun smut by night with her German Shepherd, Leo. Now, she only writes the fun smut.

Printed in Great Britain
by Amazon